PRAI

Paper

"*Paper Angels* captures the true essence of The Salvation Army Angel Tree program and the true spirit of Christmas, which is sharing and caring. I am pleased to recommend it to everyone as an inspirational story, for parents not only to share with their children but also to create a Christmas tradition for years to come."

—Lt. Col. Charles White, Salvation Army officer
and founder of the Angel Tree program

"Jimmy Wayne has used his God-given talent for songwriting to craft *Paper Angels,* an inspired and beautifully written timeless story that will bless and encourage you to make a difference. Like other classic tales of Christmas, this one should be read year after year as a reminder of why we celebrate and give."

—Ron Hall, *New York Times* bestselling
author of *Same Kind of Different as Me*

"Jimmy Wayne has taken the pathos, poignancy, heart, and storytelling abilities that infuse his music and translated them into a novel that will inspire all those who read it to take the first step toward making a difference."

—Jennifer Perry, executive director,
Children's Action Network

Rhoda Borchardt
October 2014

Paper Angels

A Novel

Jimmy Wayne

– *with* –

TRAVIS THRASHER

New York Nashville London Toronto Sydney New Delhi

Howard Books
A Division of Simon & Schuster, Inc.
1230 Avenue of the Americas
New York, NY 10020

This book is a work of fiction. Names, characters, places, and incidents either are products of the author's imagination or are used fictitiously. Any resemblance to actual events or locales or persons, living or dead, is entirely coincidental.

First Howard Books hardcover edition November 2011

HOWARD and colophon are trademarks of Simon & Schuster, Inc.

For information about special discounts for bulk purchases, please contact Simon & Schuster Special Sales at 1-866-506-1949 or business@simonandschuster.com.

The Simon & Schuster Speakers Bureau can bring authors to your live event. For more information or to book an event, contact the Simon & Schuster Speakers Bureau at 1-866-248-3049 or visit our website at www.simonspeakers.com.

Designed by Jaime Putorti

Manufactured in the United States of America

10 9 8 7 6 5 4 3 2 1

Library of Congress Cataloging-in-Publication Data

Wayne, Jimmy, 1972–
Paper angels : a novel / Jimmy Wayne with Travis Thrasher.—1st Howard books hardcover ed.
p. cm.
1. People with social disabilities—North Carolina—Fiction. 2. Christian life—Fiction. 3. Salvation Army—Fiction. 4. Christmas stories. 5. Domestic fiction. I. Thrasher, Travis, 1971– II. Title.
PS3623.A958P37 2011
813'.6—dc22
2011016283

ISBN 978-1-4516-0619-5
ISBN 978-1-4516-0620-1 (ebook)

To Bea and Russell Costner

There wouldn't be me if there hadn't been you.

Paper Angels

Preface

When his mom decided it was time for them to leave and leave for good, Thomas knew they better get far away or he'd come and find them. The good thing or the bad thing, depending on how one looked at it, was that it was Christmas day and food was still cooking in the kitchen. Just another Christmas, with Mom sweating in a tiny room over a tiny stove, Thomas and Sara dreaming of the iPods or gaming equipment they could be enjoying, and Dad watching college basketball on his flat-screen television and drinking with a vengeance. This was the worst time they could possibly ever leave, and that was what made it the best.

"Thomas, I need your help," Mom called.

He didn't go right away, watching the game with almost as much interest as Dad. It was only when his father barked out his name that Thomas went. Dad wasn't concerned about Mom's needing help—he didn't want any interruptions to his game. It would sure help them all out if the UNC Tarheels would score a little more often. Thomas got up, figuring he needed to take out the garbage or Benny, his dad's dog.

"I want you to do something and not ask any questions, do you understand?" Mom's voice was barely audible over the sound of the stove's fan.

"What do you mean?"

"I want you to get your sister and go out to the car, okay?"

Right there and then he knew. Something was wrong. The way his mother looked and sounded today seemed different. The bruise above her lips was still swollen, but that wasn't anything new. It was the look in her eyes, a look he'd never seen before.

"Where are we going?"

"Get Sara and take her to the car right now."

He nodded. The smell of the sweet potatoes and the ham and the fresh biscuits and the macaroni pie all made his mouth water. But fear made his hunger go quiver in a corner.

Thomas wanted to ask his mother but he knew. The knowing part of him whispered for his mouth to stay shut and for his legs to start moving.

Getting Sara would be easy. In fact, doing anything now would be easy except taking Dad's can of Coors Light away from him or turning off his game.

He was able to get his sister's attention without a problem. She looked up when he came into the living room. She was eleven but she tried to act older. For a moment he mouthed that she needed to come, signaling for her to follow him. The game no longer interested him. All he could think about was his mother's request.

"What do you think you're doing?" his father asked.

Thomas hadn't seen his father looking at him. Usually by now, about three-fourths of the way into the basketball game, he was in a semicoma that would only to be broken by another trip to the fridge.

"Every time you wave your arms Benny thinks you're playing with him. So knock it off. Unless you're going to take him outside for a walk."

"Yes, sir."

Sara didn't need an explanation to follow into the other room. Dad's tone was enough. Once inside the kitchen, Thomas guided her toward the back door.

"We need to go," he said outside.

"Go where?"

"Away"

"Where's that? I'm hungry." They walked quickly out the door and to the car.

The first thing Thomas thought of as he climbed into the musty-smelling Nissan was his bike.

The bike that he and Mom had finally saved up enough to buy, a used and recycled mountain bike that they'd spent a hundred and fifty bucks on. A bike that when new would have cost over a thousand. A bike that had seen better days but still had some life in it.

Maybe not much of a life after all.

Thomas thought about what to do about the bike. It was getting rusty and the paint was chipped but he still loved it. Maybe he could ride it and follow behind the car. Or maybe they could fit it in the fifteen-year-old Maxima.

They waited in the car for ten minutes. Ten whole minutes.

He sat in the front seat looking at the small house with the wild shrubs growing unevenly around it and the rusted-out white truck that couldn't fit all of them in the front seat.

"What are we doing?" Sara kept asking.

"We're waiting for Mom."

"Where are we going?"

"Far away."

Mom had told them—no, she'd *promised* them—that they would be getting a special Christmas present today. Just the two kids. She had said she would give it to them during the day, that it was going to be a surprise, that they couldn't mention it to Dad. *This is her present,* Thomas thought as he waited and worried that the next one out of the house would be the man with the glassy eyes and the tightened jaw. His hands felt sweaty as he rubbed them and tried to act like he wasn't nervous in front of his sister.

Maybe she planned on leaving later. Maybe the fight they had when she started cooking dinner convinced her to go now.

The door opened and Thomas stopped breathing.

It was Mom.

All she carried was her purse. Maybe she had already packed a few things, but he didn't see anything in the backseat.

How do I ask her about my bike?

As she climbed into the car, Thomas could see the fear on her face and in the way she moved. Before starting up the car, she turned to face both of them.

"You two, listen to me. We're leaving and we're not coming back, and I'll explain why. But for now we have to go. Do you understand me?"

Sara began asking questions, but it was Thomas who told her to be quiet, not Mom.

He didn't need to be told why.

He didn't need to ask about his bike either.

The car left without hesitation.

Thomas and Sara had received the best gift ever: freedom.

The question was whether it would still be there tomorrow and the next day and the day after that.

And whether the man inside the house they were leaving would find them and reclaim them as his own.

God Must Be a Country Music Fan

The snow dancing on the sidewalk alongside the towering skyscraper reminded Kevin Morrell of better days, when he walked here with his wife celebrating a new year and a new business and a thousand new opportunities. A decade later, the snow still circled his feet and the city still searched for its pot of gold, but Kevin walked alone, knowing he was down to one single chance.

He wished Jenny was here. Something about her presence always gave him more confidence. She had been the first to tell him to take a leap of faith, to quit the corporate job and become his own boss. The look in her eyes had told him he could do that.

Kevin could use that look right now.

For a moment, before crossing the street and entering the skyscraper to find out the verdict on his next year, Kevin stopped for a moment and took a few deep breaths. He didn't want to admit he was nervous, but every bone in his body felt it. He wanted to appear cool and collected, as if this meeting didn't mean everything, as if keeping this retainer wasn't a matter of making or breaking him. Kevin wanted to appear in control.

Staring up into the sky on this chilly day before Thanksgiving in New York City, Kevin knew he didn't control anything anymore.

*

Twenty-five or thirty presents waited under the glittering Christmas tree in the corner of the lobby. Kevin had been staring at the gifts for some time now, wondering whether there were actual items in the wrapped boxes or if they were just for show. He thought the latter, especially since he doubted a company like Silverschone Investments got together to pick names and sip hot cocoa and play warm and fuzzy Christmas games.

Warm *and* fuzzy *aren't the words I'd associate with anything to do with banks or mortgages these days.*

He thought it was interesting to have the Christmas tree out before Thanksgiving. Perhaps the decorating committee was on top of things this year. Or maybe they knew the company was going to go under before Christmas, so best celebrate the season as quickly as possible.

Stop with the stupid thoughts, Kev. His lower back was starting to sweat. Maybe because after sitting in this fancy leather armchair for what felt like forever, he was beginning to feel strapped into a straitjacket. Or maybe because he wasn't used to wearing a dress shirt and a coat. This was as dressy as he got, unless someone died or got married.

Kevin Morrell was able to set the dress code at his office,

and that meant business casual with a stress on the word *casual*. No, he didn't want people showing up in flip-flops and looking as if they just came from the beach or were on their way to a Jimmy Buffett concert. But he also hated the corporate thing.

To try to combat the nervous energy that made him cross his legs a dozen times, Kevin took out his phone and logged onto Twitter. This was his guilty pleasure, like Jenny's love of chocolate, which had recently been doubly intensified. After reading tweets from strangers commenting on politics and pop culture and how long it took to get out of a parking garage, Kevin decided to share what had been on his mind for the past half hour.

I'm wondering what this receptionist really does, because for half an hour I've seen nothing going on except Nazi-like stares.

He had thirteen more characters to spare. Awesome.

Maybe she's following you on Twitter and she goes by GuardTheDoor911.

He deleted the stupid tweet before posting it, and then stuck his phone back into his pocket. He thought of a joke he'd heard a while ago about a man phoning a mental institution. The caller asks the receptionist to check and see if there is anybody in room 24. When the receptionist tells the man the room is empty, he says, "Good, that means I really did escape."

Now I'm telling myself jokes. This meeting needs to happen before I start getting really loopy.

Kevin breathed in and out slowly, a technique he used whenever he was about to speak to a large group or go into an intense meeting.

The door finally opened and Dan walked through, shaking his head and rolling his eyes.

"Man, I'm so sorry you had to wait."

"It's okay," Kevin said, smiling as if he hadn't spent the better part of an hour twiddling and tweeting his thumbs.

They shook hands and Dan nodded for him to follow. They'd met like this many times, but something felt different. Everything from the plane ride here to waiting in the lobby for so long to Dan's quickly ushering him inside.

I'm just being paranoid.

"We had to have a meeting right before everybody took off for Thanksgiving," Dan said as he walked to his office. "What a joke."

"Everything okay?"

Dan gave a half laugh as they took their seats, Dan behind the desk and Kevin in front. Kevin had noted how busy people outside Dan's office seemed, busier than he'd ever seen them. Inside the office, Dan's big body tilted back in a chair that appeared beaten into submission.

"So how are you doing?" Dan asked it like a counselor, in a tone that wanted to know if he was about ready to jump out a fifty-first-story window.

"Doing well."

"Trip up here good?"

Kevin nodded as he shifted in his seat. He already knew the answer he'd been dreading. He wasn't being Debbie Downer, but he knew. Dan's serious glance, his tone, the awkward small talk.

"Jenny feeling okay?"

"Yeah. Sure. She keeps getting more uncomfortable but that's part of the process."

"When are the babies due again?"

"Technically February but we're now thinking it'll be more like January. Hoping, at least."

Hoping for a lot of things, Dan.

"Wow. And what are you having?"

"Two more boys."

Dan nodded and raised his eyebrows in a manner that said, *You're in deep, buddy.* He didn't need to tell him. Kevin knew too well.

"You ready for the twins?"

"I don't know if anybody is ever ready for one, much less two."

"See, that's why I never married," Dan said as he glanced down at his desk and pulled over a document. "Then I'd be sitting there like you—one with two more on the way. I can barely manage owning a dog."

Speaking of dogs, the hot dog Kevin had grabbed at the airport for lunch no longer seemed like a sensible, time-saving decision. Now it was barking somewhere deep down inside of his gut.

"I don't know how to tell you this."

Boom.

"That's the opening line of every bad piece of news there is," Kevin said.

"Man, this isn't personal, you know."

Sure is to me, buddy.

Kevin nodded and kept his mouth shut. He wiped the sweat off his forehead.

"We're not going to be able to renew the retainer," Dan said, looking at the document that was surely the one Kevin was hoping to sign and bring back home to Jenny and the boys. "I know we've been talking and I've been telling you it looked promising. And it did for a while . . ."

Kevin moved to the edge of his seat, not looking away from Dan and not blinking. "Can you tell me why?"

"You're expensive," Dan said, his blunt New York style adding to the blow.

"As I told you before, the retainer price can be renegotiated if you want—"

"No, Kevin. I'm sorry. It's not that. Entire budgets have been slashed including marketing and PR. They've given me nothing to work with. There's no way we can keep a firm on a retainer. I'm working project by project. And even those are going to be dramatically different."

Kevin's mind raced. As he swallowed, his mouth and throat felt dry. Even though he usually thought the worst, actually experiencing it was a blow.

"Is there anything I can do?" he asked. "Anything to change your mind?"

Dan rubbed his cheek. He looked a lot like Kevin probably looked: overworked, underpaid, stressed out. "It's not *my* mind that needs to change. I tried, Kevin. You gotta believe me. I really did—I know with your family and all—"

"No, it's okay," Kevin said.

My family and the twins are my business, and that's none of your concern.

Dan gritted his teeth, glancing down at his desk for an awkward moment. Kevin didn't realize that his last statement had come out so loud, so aggressive sounding.

"Maybe there will be a chance to have Precision work with you guys in the coming year on some of those projects," Kevin said, trying to control his voice and his expression and his pride.

"Yeah, maybe."

It was like a girl telling him they could still be friends just after dumping him.

"I hate doing this right before the holidays," Dan said.

Oh yeah, make that like being dumped before prom.

Dan studied him, could no doubt see the surprise on his face.

"I didn't want to do this over the phone," he said, his look earnest. "I was really hoping to change minds or I never would have had you fly all the way out here."

"I understand. Really."

"It's tough for everybody these days."

Kevin nodded, forced a smile, and then shifted, ready to bolt. The last thing he wanted was to be talked down to in pity.

"I appreciate your business," Kevin said. "It's meant a lot."

He stood and shook hands with Dan.

There was one thing he'd learned years ago. Don't burn a bridge. Especially when that bridge accounted for most of his revenue.

The walk back to the not-so-friendly receptionist felt excruciating. Yet in a strange way, Kevin felt he'd rather be there under her Nazi rule than enduring Dan's sympathetic, sad stare.

A large hand clapped his shoulder in a way that surely was intended as brotherly. Instead, it made Kevin feel like a little boy.

"Man, I'm sorry. Really, truly sorry."

Kevin nodded. "Me too. You've got my number. You know where to call if you need anything. *Anything.*"

So this is it. This is how it goes.

Dan walked back to his desk and his job and his life while Kevin stood in the lobby for a moment. He glanced at the receptionist and smiled at her. She gave a polite but quick smile, then looked back down at whatever was down there in front of her to look at.

As he passed the Christmas tree to go to the elevator, Kevin thought about taking one of the elegantly wrapped presents home with him as a reminder. Then he could open it up on Christmas morning to find the answer he'd been waiting for for several weeks.

Look, honey, this is what I spent ten years working toward.

The box would be empty, of course. Like this trip. Like his career.

As he entered the elevator, Muzak played a rendition of a country song he knew well. And it caused Kevin to start laughing, then to shake his head and look at the reflection of himself in the door in front of him.

God must be a country music fan, he thought. *'Cause this is how He gets back at me for ignoring Him for so long.*

The song that played was "He Stopped Loving Her Today" by George Jones.

And yes, that's what had happened today.

A Little Turkey Somewhere

The worst part about holes in his socks were the blisters. And the worst part about blisters was trying to play basketball with them.

Doesn't really matter much when you don't have a team to play for.

Thomas took off his shoes and then winced as he peeled off his socks. They were officially done, no doubt about it. He'd need to go to the dollar store soon and get some new ones. As he tossed the rags to his side on the living room floor, his sister moaned in protest.

"Put your socks back on!" Sara said. She sat on the couch across from him in the little trailer Mom had managed to find after they took off last Christmas.

The trailer hid in the middle of nowhere, a side road off a side road. It was right across from the Sinclair farm, so there was always a nice smell in the air at any given point of the day. Barbed wire highlighted the edges of the property, though the trailer they were renting belonged to the Sinclair family, as did much of the land surrounding them.

Sometimes Thomas felt like they had stumbled upon this place and that any minute now someone was going to come storming in telling them they had no right to be there.

"Just hush," he said, too tired to deal with Sara's annoyance right now.

"What are we doing for lunch?"

"I don't know."

"You know the stove's not working again." Sara sounded like an adult, like it was his fault and he should do something immediately.

"Guess we can't cook the turkey, then."

She obviously wasn't in the mood for his jokes. "Mom's working."

"I know."

He knew well. That was one reason he'd played ball this morning. Wasn't much else to do. It was that, or stay home in the trailer listening to his annoying little sister.

"We have to eat, you know."

"No we don't," Thomas told her, still trying to joke.

"It's Thanksgiving."

"Really?"

When it was just the two of them, Sara acted like a baby. It wasn't just what she said but the tone she used. Obviously she hadn't inherited Mom's toughness.

"What are we going to eat?"

"Did you look in the fridge?" he asked.

"Yeah."

"What'd you find?"

"Not much."

"Well, that stinks."

"Tommy."

She was the only one who called him that. Some of the kids back home used to, but even his mother called him Thomas now. As if he were grown up since they'd been away from Dad for almost a year and he was the man of the family. He didn't mind Sara calling him Tommy. It sort of reminded him of something normal and nice.

"I'll figure something out," he said.

"Why didn't you get us lunch when you were gone?"

"I was playing basketball."

"So?"

"What'd you want me to do? Shoot a bear?"

"I'm hungry."

"Well, I am too. Do you have any money?"

"I never have any money."

Her whine level was especially high today.

"So what's the plan?"

When he took his time in answering, Sara obviously decided she'd had enough. She went back to her room, which was the size of a walk-in closet more than anything else. There she'd probably do the same thing he often found himself doing in the small living area of the trailer: sitting, thinking, feeling cooped up and bored. The family had only a tiny television with a few basic channels to watch with no video games to play or even a phone to make calls.

Thomas looked around, wondering where the smell came from. It wasn't his feet. This particular scent had been there since they moved in. It seriously smelled like a dead animal had found this run-down shell and decided to die underneath it.

Mom liked to say that this broken-down trailer was an answer to prayer, but prayers had to smell a lot better than this.

Then again, maybe it *was* his feet. And if it was, then he needed more than new socks.

He thought about the lunch dilemma and had an idea.

*

Half an hour later, they had a feast on the table.

"What is that?" Sara stood back, her arms crossed in front of her.

Thomas smiled, knowing that'd be the response from his sister.

"*That* is our Thanksgiving dinner."

For a moment he wondered whether Sara was going to stay at the table or go back to her room.

"Where's the turkey?" she asked.

"There." He pointed at the plate in the middle of the table.

"Those are hot dogs."

"I'm sure there's probably a little turkey somewhere in them."

Sara sighed and stared at him.

"Hey—that's not a very thankful spirit, is it?"

"I could've made those myself." She wrinkled up her nose even though there wasn't anything bad to smell. "We don't even have buns."

"Uh-uh," he said, shushing her.

She wasn't going to wreck his good mood.

"Look, we have turkey. This is our stuffing."

"Those are Cheetos."

He shrugged. "Okay, it's magical stuffing, then. This, of course, is our macaroni pie."

Sara couldn't seem to help the smile dawning on her face. "That's macaroni and cheese. We had that last night."

"These are our sweet potatoes."

"Those are those gross yogurt-covered pretzels Mom brought home."

"You never eat sweet potatoes anyway, right?"

"Tommy."

He pulled a chair out for her, now totally acting the part of the host and the cook. "I got you sweet tea to drink. And just wait for dessert."

Sara sat down and then asked for some mustard.

"You put mustard on turkey?" he joked with her. "That's a new one."

She laughed as he put the mustard in front of her.

"What if I could magically make this actually turn into a Thanksgiving feast?"

"That'd be awesome," she said.

Thomas sat down and then closed his eyes and held his breath. He held it as long as he could, turning red and feeling a little dizzy.

When he opened them again, Sara was looking at him like he'd lost his mind.

"What are you doing?"

"I tried," he said. "Nope. Can't do it."

The moment of her amusement had passed and now she was starting to grow cool and above it all again.

"Okay, look—let me pray for this. Our wonderful meal." Thomas closed his eyes and began, "Dear Jesus, thanks for this food, and thanks for our family. Please be with Mom as she's working. Help her to have a good, uh—a great day, and bless us. And just help—just be with Dad wherever he is. Amen."

As he opened his eyes, Thomas took a couple hot dogs and started eating before noticing his sister.

"What now?" he eventually asked.

"Why'd you say that?"

"Say what?"

"Say that. About Dad."

He shrugged, finishing the bite he just took. "I don't know."

"He's not our dad anymore, you know."

"Can't change that," Thomas said. "I figured best thing to do is to pray for him. Maybe it'll help."

"You really think so?"

Thomas nodded and took another big bite.

They finished the four hot dogs in just a matter of minutes. When they did, Thomas and Sara stared at each other.

"Okay, I'm still hungry," Sara said.

The macaroni and cheese had gone untouched. Both of them were sick of macaroni and cheese.

"You know—I do have a little money stored away for an emergency," Thomas said. "Think this is an emergency?"

"I've been hungry all day."

My li'l sis, the drama queen.

"Okay. Fine. But only if you promise to cheer up."

Headed for Two Giant Glaciers

Sometimes being an adult was about faking it, and that was what Kevin was doing with this turkey. He'd never officially been responsible for cooking one before. It was one of the duties he'd taken over from Jenny so she could avoid doing too much work for Thanksgiving dinner. As he leaned over the island in the middle of the kitchen with the electric knife in his hand, he hoped it wouldn't end up like that turkey in *National Lampoon's Christmas Vacation*. The movie was a standard in the Morrell household during the month of December, so he didn't want to hear any references to a gasping turkey letting out its final breath because of his poor cooking.

"How's it look?" Jenny asked as she studied it from the other side of the island.

Kevin took a bite and feigned bliss.

It's actually pretty good.

"No problem," he said to his wife. "I thought you were supposed to be resting."

"I'm fine. I'm just making sure we haven't forgotten anything."

"You mean *I* haven't forgotten anything."

"No, Mom was working on some items too."

He grinned as he watched Jenny checking the various pots on the stove. The perfectionist couldn't help herself, especially when her mother was around. Jenny's mother loved helping out but she also loved playing with Gregory. Sometimes she'd start playing with her grandson and ignore dinner altogether.

"It's fine," he said over the sound of the knife. "You've been on your feet too much this morning."

"I'm fine," she said.

But her pretty little face said differently. He could see that Jenny was tired. She passed by him and opened the fridge. With her back to him, Jenny didn't even look pregnant. She was all belly at thirty weeks, even though she constantly complained how big she was getting and she constantly ignored his comments about how beautiful she looked.

"Jen?"

"What?" She wasn't getting anything in the fridge, just making sure everything was in order.

"We've got it covered."

She glanced at him and then smiled. "Okay."

"It's fine. Now just relax."

"It's hard to do that when everybody's coming over."

"It'll be fine."

As she walked back into the family room, he kept carving the turkey.

Relax . . . It'll be fine . . .

He could say these words to her even if he didn't believe them himself.

Sometime today after the meal and after everybody was gone, he'd have to tell his wife the truth. But it was Thanksgiving, and he didn't want her worrying.

I'll tell her later. I'll figure out a way.

*

The best part of the day for Kevin and Jenny was just after they got Gregory to bed when they had a few minutes to themselves. The problem lately was that both of them were usually too exhausted by then to appreciate it.

Tonight was no different. The busyness of Thanksgiving was over but no one had recovered from the festivities. Jenny probably should have already been in bed but she was fighting sleep while lying on the couch and watching television. She didn't have to tell Kevin how uncomfortable she was. He could tell just by the way she lay there and by the expression on her face.

"You never did say how the meeting yesterday went."

They'd had a full house today, with both sets of parents and siblings over. In the chaos of about ten adults and a dozen children, it was easy for Kevin and Jenny not to connect.

Part of him wished this conversation could wait for tomorrow. But that was part of the problem the last few years. Every conversation and every special occasion and every intimate connection always seemed to be put on hold for tomorrow, for whenever he was wasn't busy. "It was fine," he said.

This is the last thing she needs right now.

Jenny nodded as she gazed back at the television, shifting uncomfortably on the couch. Every day Kevin was reminded that no matter how much he had to cope with, he still had the easier job of the two of them. Moving around the house, especially up and down the stairs, was becoming quite a chore for his wife. He couldn't imagine what it would be like carrying *one* baby inside of him, but two really blew his mind. Each day this realization shook him a little more, both with a joy he was afraid to fully embrace and with a panic he was afraid Jenny would finally see.

Having their first hadn't been easy. They were both in their early thirties before deciding to try for a child. Then, after a couple of years with no results, Kevin and Jenny met with a fertility doctor. Thankfully, after going through tests, they were given the green light for IUI. Kevin still had trouble remembering what that stood for, but he knew one of the words was *insemination*. Unlike so many other couples that struggled through a long and difficult process, theirs had worked on the second try.

That second try had resulted in their life-loving little boy. Kevin couldn't imagine life without the four-year-old.

Because Gregory's delivery had been a difficult one, with him coming out initially not breathing, doctors were monitoring Jenny's progress with the twins constantly. Now Jenny was thirty-nine. The twins were growing steadily—Kevin and Jenny were thankful for that—but they still carried some concern over Baby B. That was what they called the babies, Baby A and Baby B. B was significantly smaller than A. Each visit to measure the babies' growth caused Jenny's worry to grow a little. Kevin's grew too, but he tried his best to keep those fears from her.

"So what exactly does *fine* mean?" Jenny asked. She was looking at him.

"*Fine* means it was fine. It wasn't great."

Even an exhausted and pregnant and highly hormonal Jenny was perceptive enough to see through his vague answer.

Sometimes I wish she didn't know me so well.

Her blue eyes locked onto his in a fully awake glance. "What happened?"

"We didn't sign a contract."

Her blond hair spilled over on one shoulder as she shifted and sat up on the couch. "Are you serious?"

"I knew it was a possibility before I went."

Jenny waited for him to say more but more wasn't coming. There wasn't a lot to say.

"What are you going to do?"

He hated seeing the anxiety on her pretty face. "It's going to be fine. Just trust me. Okay? Our minivan is big enough for all of us to sleep inside."

"That's not funny."

Kevin took a sip of his wine. "Look, it's okay. I'm totally equipped to deliver both the babies if I have to. I mean—look at the job I did on the turkey."

This put a smile on Jenny's face. His humor was one of the things that she said had made her fall in love with him. It was also one of the things that had been absent for some time in their house.

"I've got to figure some things out, but I can't exactly do that now," he told her.

Not that I've ever been prevented from figuring things out late into the night on so many other projects.

"Are you still going shopping tomorrow?" she asked.

"Of course."

"You don't have to."

"No. Jen, I promised."

"But things are different."

He noticed neither of them was paying attention to the reality show on television, so he turned it off. "That's what we said last year."

"But you don't have to."

"No, I'm going and that's it. Your mom said she could look after Gregory if you want to get out."

"I'm not worried about that. I just don't want you spending money we don't have."

Jenny's tired expression now was full of worry. This was exactly what he had wanted to avoid. She didn't need any extra stress, especially stress caused by him.

"Hey—if the rest of the country can spend money they don't have, why can't I?"

Jenny didn't smile this time.

He sat down beside her and put an arm around her. "It'll be fine, okay? I won't spend much."

"You shouldn't spend anything."

"You tell me that, yet you keep buying things for the twins."

"That was before I knew this," Jenny said. "Besides, everything I get is on sale."

"So I'll look for stuff on sale tomorrow."

"I don't *need* anything."

He looked at Jenny. She was so beautiful. He didn't tell her because she would say he was crazy like she always did, but it was true. It wasn't just the cliché of her glowing throughout her pregnancy. It was more than that.

She looks young. She doesn't look like someone less than a year away from forty.

Then again, what was a woman who was almost forty and expecting twins supposed to look like?

Jenny waited to see if he would say anything else, but then said she was fried and needed to get to bed. He smiled and told her he'd stay up for a while to watch television even though there was nothing he wanted to watch. After he turned on ESPN, his thoughts were filled with everything he needed to do. Then he thought of what she had said about her not needing anything.

Yeah, you need a husband who can tell you you're beautiful without feeling awkward or waiting for the right time *to say it.*

He couldn't remember how long it had been since he'd been able to tell Jenny every waking thought he had, how long he'd been able to relax in her arms and not worry. He'd tried to keep his worry from her, but in doing so he'd managed to keep other things too. Now sometimes it seemed like they were headed toward this giant glacier and they were on two separate ships.

Make that headed for two giant glaciers. Baby A and Baby B.

For a long time, in the silence of the living room, Kevin wondered what kind of life the twins would have alongside their big brother. He wanted to believe that everything was going to be okay, that he would be able to provide the way any other father would. The future, however, remained very cloudy.

4

A Dead End

Lynn Brandt held the sheet in her hand and felt a wave of anger seep through her. It was anger at her husband, at whoever taught him to drink, at herself for ever falling for the side of him that the drinking had managed to suffocate over the years. It was anger at the fact that she was having—no, she was *needing* help from others. It was anger at this dead-end road she and the kids were traveling down.

It had taken everything in her earlier today to go to the Salvation Army to sign up for their Angel Tree program. She had hoped she could get a decent-paying job by now in order to manage to get by, but she was lucky simply to have this waitressing job that occasionally paid the bills. She'd never really thought of having to do something on her own, not when she was with Daryl. At first passion had ruled their relationship. It was passion that had produced Thomas, passion that had forced them to marry in the first place. But soon it was replaced by other strong emotions. Tension. Anger. Resentment.

Never once had Lynn thought she might need to plan for this life, trying to support two kids on her own. She was still at a crossroads. Should she divorce Daryl once and for all? Go to court and try to get child support and allow him to come back in their lives? She was afraid that she didn't have the money and the soul to go down that road. All she had wanted was to get away for a while. *A while* had ended up being almost a year now.

Maybe you better get some kind of plan in order.

Lynn kept telling herself, *In another month.* January had rolled over into February. Winter had blossomed to spring. She had kept saying, *I'll give it another week to decide on Daryl.* But her shame and her fears kept her from doing anything.

Shame and fears and, oh yeah, love.

She was ashamed to admit that she still loved a man who hit her.

He never hits really hard.

She was ashamed that she still made stupid excuses like that.

Lynn didn't want to think about contacting Daryl, about officially ending his relationship with his children. He had to be furious with her. She didn't know. Maybe he'd forgotten about her and the kids, maybe even found someone else. Part of her was afraid to find out the truth.

So with all this dragging after her like a string of clanking cans attached to her ankles making a racket every time she managed to move, Lynn had gotten nowhere trying to find a steady, good-paying job. And she'd finally given in today with the visit to the Salvation Army. The place that produced all those men and women ringing bells and asking for donations. The people who came up with the idea to put Christmas trees up in public places for kids who wouldn't be receiving presents under their own tree at home.

Now this.

For a moment she thought about bringing the information sheet on the soup kitchen back home . . . just in case.

Just in case I let them down.

But that was just for a moment. Lynn ripped the flyer into shreds so small it would be impossible to piece it back together. It was one thing to sign up for Christmas presents, but it was another to receive free food. They weren't homeless and living on the streets.

Not yet.

Lynn buried the thought and knew she was just tired and sad she couldn't be with Thomas and Sara today. As she sipped the cup of coffee she was holding, she thought how good a cigarette would taste. But she gave that up. Just like other bad things in her life.

The tiny room she sat in resembled more of a closet than the restaurant's break room. Every time she moved, her chair would rock from one side to the other. The coffee didn't work. She needed something stronger, but anything stronger than this sludge she poured for unfortunate patrons all day would be illegal. Which, considering the lousy day she'd had, didn't seem like the worst thing in the world, though all Lynn wanted to do was get home and make sure the kids were okay.

Happy Thanksgiving, she thought bitterly. *Can't wait to see the Merry Christmas we're going to have.*

The torn strips of paper from the brochure her boss had given her littered the table. Murphy had done it out of kindness, but still it had offended her. Back in Georgia, they never had money, it seemed. But now . . . now everything was different. Now her boss was right. They might just want a nice, decent meal that happened to be free.

"We're fine, thank you very much," she had said shortly.

But for a while Lynn did consider it.

Sara was always complaining about one thing or another ever since they'd moved. Her new school, their little trailer in the middle of nowhere, her lack of friends, even the lack of food in their pantry.

We're the fattest country in the world, with something like a quarter of the people considered obese, yet my daughter complains about being hungry.

Thomas was a different story. He was a growing boy who didn't need to tell her he needed more food. It was written all over his lanky body. He ate whatever generic items she had at home and did it without complaining.

A nice big meal that happened to be free wouldn't be such a bad thing.

But no, she still wasn't bringing them to any soup kitchen in the middle of Greenville. They weren't homeless and they weren't helpless. They weren't drug addicts or alcoholics. They'd just had a little run of bad luck. That was all.

She was the mother and it was her duty to take care of the essentials, stuff like food and shelter. Christmas gifts were extra, and it was okay to let others help them out with a little extra something. That's why she'd signed up for the Angel Tree program.

Not to mention the fact that no one has to see them opening those presents, isn't that right?

Her boss yelled at her from the kitchen and Lynn stood up, draining the last bit of coffee. For a moment she thought about the program she'd signed up for that brought Christmas to their home for no charge.

All that was required was the goodness of strangers. That and a visit down to the local Salvation Army so they could make sure she was who she said she was.

Going there and giving her information had been humiliating enough. Tomorrow she would talk to Sara and Thomas about what gifts they'd like. A part of her still doubted they'd actually get the things the kids would ask for. Goodness in people was nice in theory, just like marriages and soup kitchens and happily-ever-afters. But in reality, reliance on them could end up hurting you.

Hurting you and breaking your heart.

✶

The trailer looked abandoned and discarded on the side of the road.

If Lynn didn't know her children, she might think they'd abandoned and discarded her. But she knew them well—they weren't going anywhere without her.

She turned off her car and wondered, as the door squeaked open, how much longer she'd be able to drive it. Japanese cars often survived two hundred thousand miles. It was the lack of maintenance that worried her. Lynn pushed the thought from her mind.

Another day done, Lynn thought. *Another day the car did its job.*

She wished she could say the same about herself as a mom.

It was close to midnight. She still smelled like the restaurant. Sometimes she swore she could smell it even when she had freshly showered and wore different clothes. Something about the grills and the grease seemed to stick on her. Like bad memories, they wouldn't go away.

She tried the door handle to the trailer and was relieved to see it was locked. Thomas remembered.

I ask too much of him, Lord. Way too much.

Lynn was quiet as she slipped through the door and turned on the haggard light over the tiny table in the kitchen to her right. The sight depressed her, even more than the steaming grills of the diner and the gap-toothed grin of Larry, who liked to gawk at her as he slaved over them.

In the silence, she took in her surroundings and wondered again how she'd arrived at this moment. This wasn't a situation she'd suddenly walked into. This was the dead end she'd journeyed to over time.

She put her keys on the counter, then saw the note.

Hey Mom—

Leftover pizza. Found a great deal so I got us one today for Thanksgiving. Sara was happy for five seconds!

T

With that, Lynn started to cry.

Not out of self-pity or sadness. But because she'd just been reminded that this wasn't a dead end.

This trailer didn't define her. The faded and cracking walls didn't paint a picture of her or her family. This address didn't imprison her.

All of this was a starting point. It was square one.

And the note in her hand—that was the hope.

Those two children are my definition and my picture and my sanctuary.

She wiped her eyes, hoping that Thomas or Sara wouldn't come out of the darkness and see her tears. She opened the refrigerator and found the pizza.

Some people might think that struggling financially meant not buying a new coat for Christmas or not taking that vacation. But this—*this* right in her hand was what the struggle looked like, a teenage boy spending what little money he had on food.

But one thing she didn't have to look hard for was affection.

Even though she failed to show it every day, it was shown to her.

The love of kids who didn't quite understand what it even meant.

"Thank you, Lord," she said before biting into the cold pepperoni. It wasn't just the pizza she was thankful for, and He certainly knew it.

White-Trash Redneck

All eyes watched him as Thomas held the basketball, all fully aware that whoever scored next would win.

Dribbling the basketball felt as natural to Thomas as breathing or blinking. He'd grown up with a basketball in his hands, even—according to his mother—when he was just a baby and was given a soft, stuffed miniature basketball to play with. It was because of his father, of course. Dad loved the game and loved playing. Maybe he'd even been good at it at one point in his life. Thomas didn't know. He just knew it had been the one and only thing that he and his father had shared. The love of playing, of watching the UNC Tarheels win and Duke Blue Devils lose, of watching the NBA and each having his own favorite player.

Moving had meant he wouldn't be playing varsity ball at his old high school. Instead, he had to sit out this season because of the rules at Greer High. Something about kids transferring schools and unfair advantages and all that. It had been just another way being a new student made him stand out and feel separate from the rest of the kids. A lot of the guys on the team at school had snubbed him, not even giving him a chance to show them how well he played. He had begun to think he might not ever play at this school. Yet over the year, in gym class and playing pickup games at local parks like now, Thomas had developed a reputation as a great player.

That brought the good and the bad out in guys he played with.

It was no longer a secret that he was fast and that he could hit the shots. But the thing that nobody could really ever fully know until midway through the game was how badly Thomas wanted to win. It went back to playing with his father, playing with intense eyes on him with orders barked at his every move. Dad had ignited a fire deep inside him, so that every time he held that ball, he had to win. He *needed* to win as if it would assure his father staying off his case. Now he played to prove that he could win at any given time.

Today was no exception.

It had all started with a simple half-court game. Some mid-day fun in the middle of the weekend at a local court. No biggie, no drama, nothing strange. It was one of the first times he'd played with some of these guys. He thought—hoped—that everything would be cool. For a while he'd actually been able to simply be a kid trying to score.

Now there was one more play. He dribbled the ball, then passed it to Nathan, who he knew would hold on to it for a few seconds then pass it back. Nathan had a hard enough time hitting a basket without anyone blocking him. Everybody knew Nathan wasn't going to take the last shot.

With the ball passed back to him as expected, Thomas surveyed the scene. Vic was all over him just like he had been all game. Thomas wanted to pass the ball below the rim and have someone do a nice little layup. A couple other guys came up to try to block him.

Vic tapped him on the arm, an obvious foul, but he'd been doing that all day too. As a guard on the varsity team at Greer, Vic obviously had something to prove.

With two others close to him, Thomas backed over and then bolted past them. Vic trailed but was too slow.

Just as they thought he was going to drive hard to the net, Thomas backed out of the box and went up to make a shot. Vic could only do one thing—come crashing into him. But Thomas was too fast, launching a shot that would have been a three-pointer right before having his arms crushed.

The shot was a thing of beauty.

As it dropped into the net, a chorus of both cheers and "oohs" sounded. Nobody could believe that he'd been able to make it. Especially the red-faced, out-of-breath Vic.

Thomas smiled, which probably only made things worse. He couldn't help it. The guy had obviously fouled him on purpose, but Thomas kept his mouth shut.

"So where you from again?"

The comment had come as Thomas was walking off the court with some guys he thought might become friends. He certainly wouldn't mind finding a few at the high school.

For a moment Thomas didn't even realize Vic was talking to him.

"Hey, Kobe, I'm talking to you."

The other guys stopped, so Thomas did too. He turned around and saw Vic walking toward him.

"Where'd you learn to play like that?" he asked.

Where does anybody learn to play? Thomas had thought. *You just play. A lot. And if you're lucky, you can drain shots to win the game.*

"I don't know. Just played a lot."

Thomas knew he could probably say anything and still manage to get attitude from this guy who definitely didn't like losing.

"So you play a lot but you're too good to play at Greer?"

"I just started going here this year. I couldn't try out for the team. They wouldn't let me."

"You always get away with trash like that in games?"

Thomas shook his head. He might not be the best student in the world, but he knew when trouble was barking at him.

"Look, it was a good game."

"Yeah, after your ten fouls."

Is he talking about my fouls or his own?

Vic was a junior, a junior just one-upped by a sophomore. This was all about his saving face. And the more Thomas thought about Vic's face, the more he thought he resembled one of the guys on the hated Blue Devils. One of the guys Thomas and his father used to love to hate.

Leave him alone.

Thomas wasn't about to call Vic "JJ" or even say anything. But as he turned to head home, Vic had grabbed his shoulder. Thomas's instinct was to pull his shoulder roughly out of Vic's hand.

Vic's instinct, on the other hand, was to swing right for the nose, which he hit just perfectly with the first blow. Blood sprayed and the guys stood around to watch the ensuing fight or beating, whichever was about to happen.

But when Thomas stood straight from bending over as he held his gushing nose, he didn't say a word.

Vic stood there, waiting, but Thomas just walked off with Nathan and a couple other guys, making sure he didn't bleed over his clothes. One of them, a senior named Craig, gave Thomas an extra T-shirt to stop the bleeding. They asked if he was okay and said Vic was nothing but a white-trash redneck who didn't know any better.

Thomas didn't reply. He knew exactly the kind of guy Vic was. If they knew Thomas any better, they might say the same thing about him.

Strangely, Thomas felt sorry for the guy.

I'm probably just suffering from a concussion.

But he didn't think so.

Thomas knew there was probably a reason Vic was so mean. The same way his father was mean. Deep down, something was broken. They were just waiting for someone to finally come along and fix it.

*

"You need to write me a Christmas list," Mom said when he walked through the trailer door, handing him a notepad and a pen.

Thomas was chewing on a Starburst candy that tasted stale. He wondered how candy that already tasted like chewy, flavored cardboard could get so stale. Maybe that was why they were on sale for a quarter at the dollar store he stopped in on the way home from the basketball game.

"Okay," he said. "I'll take a sixty-inch TV, a satellite dish with all the college and pro games on it, and a PlayStation 3."

"I'm serious, Thomas."

"You want me to give you Christmas ideas? For me?"

"I signed Sara and you up for the Angel Tree program."

"The what?"

Thomas rubbed his nose, which he'd managed to clean up at the bathroom at the dollar store. He didn't need Mom asking him about the fight.

"The Salvation Army does a thing where kids write out what they'd like to get for Christmas and then people pick their names and buy them the presents."

"Just like that?" he asked, holding the paper and pen and suddenly feeling suspicious that Mom had signed them up for some kind of scam.

"You have to show proof that you—well, that you—"

"Have nothing?"

"That you're in need," Mom said. He was standing in the living room and she was ten feet away in the kitchen, cleaning dishes at the sink.

"So I can write anything?"

"Well, not anything," she said, glancing at him. "Just write a realistic list, things you'd want me to get you."

"You never used to get me the things I asked for."

"Why are you being so difficult today?"

Maybe because I just got socked in the nose, Mom.

"Okay, fine."

Mom didn't seem in the mood to talk. So he decided to take a shower and fill out this list.

Sure, I'll write up a list. And we'll just see if I get anything on it.

Thomas wasn't thinking about Christmas. He was still thinking about this guy named Vic, wondering what the first day back at school on Monday would bring.

Golden Ticket

All Kevin needed now was to find Wonka's Golden Ticket.

Ah, if only life could be that easy. God, you have a golden ticket to spare somewhere here in this shopping mall?

It was sarcasm, of course. Because he wasn't that bright-eyed kid he used to see mirrored in *Willy Wonka and the Chocolate Factory,* the one with Gene Wilder. And because he couldn't quite ask God for much of anything. In the long race to try to build his design and marketing firm known as Precision, God had been put in the backseat. Like everybody else. Including Jenny.

The movie had been on last night, and Kevin had watched and remembered. He felt so different from that kid who first saw it. Kevin had grown up in the Greenville area with plenty of family and friends. So when his father lost his job at the pharmaceutical company he'd worked at for over fifteen years, forcing hard times, Kevin had never truly felt the full impact as a ten-year-old. His father shifted from job to job, trying to find steady work and never quite landing back on his feet. But Kevin didn't see his youth as miserable or heartbreaking. He looked at it sorta like Charlie viewed his life in *Willy Wonka*, making the most out of the present and dreaming of a better future.

Somewhere along the way, Kevin's dream had been made reality. Perhaps that was what he feared the most, suddenly becoming a living replica of his father, who never found his footing again in life. He and Mom still lived in that small house in Greer, which he and Jenny visited often. The last thing Kevin wanted to do was show up one day and tell them that he'd lost his company, that this venture had turned out to be not such a grand adventure after all.

He sighed, wanting to take his mind off all that right now. He needed to focus and figure out something to get Jenny for Christmas.

There was a beautiful madness in the middle of this shopping mall. Impeccably dressed, finely scented, and endlessly smiling, the patrons knew this day well. They waited for it. But he was here because he needed to make amends for neglecting Christmas shopping the year before. Last year he'd waited for the last minute only to hastily buy a few gift cards that anybody could have gotten at the corner drugstore. Jenny was spending the day shopping with a friend. She would probably be tired by noon anyway.

The crowds flowing by him like a steady creek made him feel claustrophobic. Maybe it was because it had been a while since he'd come to the Haywood Mall. Or because he hadn't gone shopping on the day after Thanksgiving since . . . since he could remember. People moved like shuffling zombies, their eyes fixed on the next purchase they could devour. Kevin just wanted to find a telephone booth and close himself inside of it. Of course, pay phones were extinct in this world, not to mention the booths surrounding them.

He thought back to Christmas mornings when his parents didn't have much. Those gifts he'd received meant everything, even if he never did get an Atari like his other buddies. That was okay. Even as a kid, he knew that Dad was trying his best.

Now the promise of Christmas seemed to be more about which salesclerk made the best pitch. For a second Kevin surveyed the scene. Amid the flurry of people, he could make out the fine print.

Price tags. A number after a dollar sign. Everything in this place added up to dollars and cents. The racks of clothes and the aisles of shoes and the walls of mannequins and the posters of models all wanted to be inspected, and all tried to entice. Hope was just one transaction away. You could have a better life in just a matter of moments if you simply put down your credit card and charged away your worries.

Kevin stood near the front or the back of the store, whatever they called it, the exit that led to the rest of the mall. But it wasn't an exit to him. An exit was more like a fire escape, a door he could open to daylight and the parking lot so he could flee this mayhem. He stood looking at the people pouring in and pouring out of the department store. So much for a struggling economy. So much for a recession. Maybe people hadn't gotten the message, because they were out here in droves with hands full of stuff.

More and more stuff.

He checked his phone again out of habit and need. It was a sanity check, his security blanket.

I'm not going to find anything in here. He had scanned the store and made a couple of circles but that was like walking around a swimming pool without ever getting wet. All these others had dived in, checking out sizes and sales, trying things on. That was part of shopping, finding the good deal, finding that hidden gem amid everything else. But he didn't have the time or the patience. All he wanted to do was get out of here.

Maybe this was all wrong. Maybe there was a better strategy instead of the mall-after-Thanksgiving method. Kevin walked deeper into the store and saw an aisle of perfumes and noticed the pretty woman behind the counter talking to a customer about one of them. Jenny already had about twenty different perfumes. Some of them were so old Kevin was sure they smelled more like oblivion than Obsession.

He sighed and started to walk toward the mall side of the store when he saw it. A big tree was nearly blocking the doors. It wasn't decorated in gold and silver or red and green. Instead, it was covered in various-colored angel ornaments. Each ornament was made out of paper and contained a white slip at the bottom, a slip resembling a form someone might leave on your door handle after stopping by. Kevin slowed down and stared at it out of curiosity.

The strips of paper looked as if they had handwriting on them.

Must be a kids' project or some kind of fund-raiser.

As a father and his daughter walked up to the tree and then stood in front of it, Kevin watched. He hoped they didn't catch him gawking. The girl appeared delighted, as if she'd won a prize or something. Maybe there were prizes on the tree that somebody could pick out if they bought a certain ridiculous amount of stuff in the store. The father nodded at his daughter, who was maybe ten or so, and she carefully chose a paper angel. She studied it carefully and then read to her father whatever was written on it. Kevin was too far back to hear what the girl was saying, with the crowds and the chatter and the background music, so he moved up a little closer.

"That's great," the father told her.

Maybe she had won some designer shoes or a 40-percent-off coupon or something like that. Yet the look on the little girl's face said it was something else, something deeper.

As they started to move away from the tree, Kevin backed up and bumped into a woman who looked like she could pin him in a cage-wrestling match. The woman was large and looked very displeased.

"Excuse me, I'm sorry."

She gave him a look that said, *You should be.* Kevin grinned and wondered why he still sometimes felt like a fourteen-year-old around some people.

"Well?" she asked him in an accent that reminded him of his aunt.

Some southerners had accents, and some had *accents*. This woman fit all the stereotypes of the south except for that one big one that found her charming.

"No, sorry, go ahead," Kevin said, not sure what she was talking about.

She just shook her head and walked to the tree. The woman wore jeans that came up to her rib cage and a faded shirt that was way too small. Her hair looked desperate for a good washing.

It wasn't that Kevin was someone who judged people by their appearance—but it was a striking contrast to see someone like this amid the others in the shopping mall. A distant thought came to him when he wondered why she looked like she had just gotten out of bed.

And on the wrong side of the bed too.

The woman picked up one of the ornaments. As she turned around, she gave him a questioning look.

That's why she's here—free stuff. I knew it.

"Have a wonderful day," Kevin said, a bit too friendly, a bit too sarcastic.

He watched the lady walk off, and as he began to head outside of the store, he saw the sign.

THE SALVATION ARMY
CHRISTMAS
ANGEL TREE PROGRAM
HELP US TO HELP OTHERS BY BEING AN ANGEL
TO A NEEDY CHILD OR SENIOR CITIZEN.

Below were suggestions and guidelines for those who took the angel-shaped tags.

It took Kevin a moment to realize that the names on the tags were those of real people in real need.

Suddenly a combination of shame and guilt poured through him. Here he thought they were excited—that people could only get excited—by something free. By something selfish. But boy, was he wrong. The woman had taken an ornament so that she could help someone else.

As he stepped toward the tree, he found a card in the center of it with very neat handwriting.

There it is, man. Your Golden Ticket. Pick this and your life can change.

But he thought of everything he had going on in the coming month. Stuff with work and with Jenny and Gregory and the babies and Christmas. Kevin decided not to pick up one of the paper ornaments. Instead, he walked out of the store and decided to head back home.

It was nice to have wide-eyed hope like Charlie's when he was a kid, but he was grown-up now. And part of being a grown-up was realizing that there weren't such things as Santa Claus or reindeer or Golden Tickets that were magically going to help.

Help came when you went looking for it. Which was exactly what Kevin planned to do.

Another Not-So-Good Guy

"*Did you finish* your list?"

Mom asked this after she finished her muffin and headed back to the one bathroom they all shared in the trailer. It was Saturday and she always started work around ten.

"Not yet," he called out.

When his mother came back into the room, her hair was in a ponytail that made her look younger. He liked the way she looked. Even though she was always busy and often looked really tired, Thomas liked seeing his mother busy. Like she had a purpose. Back at home, there'd been times when she looked lost.

Make that imprisoned.

There was something different about her now. She almost seemed lighter, younger.

Freer even though she was tired.

"Make sure you fill that out today, okay?"

"Anything I want, huh?"

"No," Mom said, glancing at him with a you-know-better look. "Be reasonable."

"Hey, it's free stuff."

"Yeah, stuff that someone has to buy. Someone is giving their money to buy you presents. So within reason."

"Did Sara give you her list?"

"We need to modify it a bit."

"So does the person giving us these gifts show up at our door or something?"

"Of course," she said with amusement on her face. "They have Christmas dinner with us."

"Are we even *having* Christmas dinner?"

"We'll see."

"Last one didn't go so well."

"Don't be such a smart aleck."

Thomas laughed. "That's not what Dad calls me."

"We won't have that kind of language in this house. Not anymore. Look—I gotta go. Are you still going to see about that job?"

"Yes."

"Don't give me that tone."

Thomas sighed. "It's not like I haven't been trying."

"You haven't been trying hard enough."

"I'm going today."

"Good. I'll be home a little after dinner."

"What time?"

She looked at him, her eyebrows wrinkled and her expression surprised. "I don't know—do I have a curfew?"

"Last time 'a little after dinner' ended up being ten o'clock."

"That's why you need a job. Then you can afford to get a cell phone that I can call."

"Maybe I'll put that on my list."

"You might be surprised at what you get."

He wanted to tell her that he doubted it but instead he said good-bye and watched her open the door and leave. Here he was again, the man of the house. He wasn't quite a man yet and this wasn't quite a house, but close enough. Sara was at a friend's, a friend who probably had cable and Internet and video games. Thomas only had his latest Dennis Shore novel, but that would tide him over.

He liked reading horror stories about families much worse off than them. It made him appreciate all they had, even if it wasn't very much.

*

Blood still stained his Nikes.

Thomas noticed it as he glanced down while waiting for the Bi-Lo manager to come back. He'd forgotten to get the blood out after Vic had nailed his nose a week ago. Thankfully there hadn't been any new run-ins with Vic since.

Item number one on Mom's secret Santa list: new basketball shoes.

He wondered what would happen if he got a pair of generic shoes like the food in their pantry. Not Nike or Reebok but a new brand called Niebok! "Same cushion for a third of the price."

Beggars can't be choosers.

Mom said that often and he knew what she meant. Any kind of new shoes would be better than the ones he had, which were falling apart *and* bloody.

"Sorry for making you wait," Mr. Chandler said when he returned. "Weekend after Thanksgiving's always crazy."

"That's fine."

"It's Tom, right?"

He nodded. He let people call him Tom just to make things easier.

The balding guy scanned him in the dismissive way most adults did.

He'd actually combed his hair today but maybe that was the problem. It had been a while since he'd gotten a haircut, but since his mom cut his hair, it was like choosing between bad hair and a bad haircut. Thomas had worn his best jeans and one of the only button-down shirts he owned. But he still had an idea of what he looked like—shabby.

"Look, there's lots of kids who want bagging jobs. Wasn't too long ago that I had a problem getting anybody to apply. Times are different nowadays. I got too many on hand as of now. And working in the Farmstand is out of the question. You gotta work your way up. All I can do is keep your application on file."

"I'm a hard worker," Thomas said.

"That's good to hear. I got some real lazy ones. So you never know. I'll keep you in mind."

"Thank you," Thomas said.

"Where are you going to school?"

"Greer."

"Like it there?"

"Yeah, sure."

Thomas didn't want to tell the truth.

The truth didn't need telling. The truth was spattered across his basketball shoes.

"Why are you applying now? Why didn't you apply back in summer?"

He had spent this summer working at the Sinclair farm. The same Sinclair who owned their trailer. It had been a good-paying job that he'd hoped he could keep through the school year. But once winter came, there wasn't as much to do.

"I moved here from out of state," he said for an easy explanation even though it had been almost a year since moving.

Mr. Chandler stared at him a second, and Thomas could see it in his eyes. He'd seen this look before on some of the teachers' faces. It was the same look one gave to a dirty, lost puppy wandering the street.

After saying good-bye, Thomas left the store. He knew that if he stuck around, he might be tempted to buy something. And the five bucks he had on hand was the only money he had until next week when he worked at the Parker residence again. The Parkers were an older couple down the road who had hired him to clean up their backyard, which had ten years' worth of junk behind it. He'd already spent some of his money on the pizza for Thanksgiving. His remaining five bucks could go in a blink, so it was best that he got away from temptation.

He thought of Mr. Chandler's question about liking school. He wished he'd thought of something witty to say. Sara always seemed to have funny comebacks. Thomas had a hard time remembering a joke, much less saying something clever. When Sara wasn't acting her age, she had a funny, quirky way about her.

"I like school about as much as canned beets," his sister might have said.

She wouldn't say something that normal. She would have said something more unusual, more memorable.

Some people in life just aren't that memorable.

He thought back to his shoes and wished he could fall in that category, the overlooked and ignored one. But high school boys could be mean, Thomas knew. Bored high school boys could be downright vicious. And bored high school boys who also happened to be looking for trouble—well, those were the ones Thomas knew could be deadly.

Some might call them stupid rednecks, but then again, I might be lumped into that category.

He walked across a major road and then walked alongside the road until he reached the side street that he turned on. It was a good day for a walk. Then again, every day was a good day to walk. Better to walk than be driven around in their beat-up car or ride the school bus that made him feel like a convict heading to prison.

Does blood wash out of basketball shoes?

He bet that Jack back at his old school knew. Jack was one of his best friends and liked random facts like that. Things like when you die, your hair still grows for a couple of months. Or women blink twice as often as men. Or that the state of Florida is bigger than England. Jack would come across seemingly useless information like this and store it away. Thomas always found it amusing to see what piece of information Jack would end up revealing next.

He could hear his own breathing as he walked down the road. He could see the stains on his shoes again, the blood belonging more to a scene in some horror movie than to him.

Thomas thought back to the fight with Vic.

The more he thought of why it had happened, the more he believed it was because he was a new kid. He and Vic might have been friends if they'd grown up around each other. But nobody liked the new guy. Very few people had bothered noticing him, especially the jocks. But Vic couldn't help but notice him after that amazing shot. Now he was the new kid who looked like some poor hick but could whip it on a basketball court. Put that into a blender and press mix.

I'll just keep my distance from Vic. Nothing says I need to play ball with the guy again. It's not like I'm on the team. Yet.

He picked up a rock on the side from the road and chucked it. Thomas knew that eventually he needed to figure out how to make friends on the basketball team. If they were all like Vic, well—

Most of them are probably good guys. I just gotta be patient. Keep trying.

He started thinking of that Christmas list again when a pickup truck behind him honked its horn and forced Thomas off the road. He moved to let the vehicle pass.

But just as the truck drove by, still honking, Thomas knew.

He knew probably before the driver knew.

The brakes squealed as the truck skidded to a stop.

The red lights backing up spelled trouble, but Thomas didn't even see them.

He was already running down the street in the opposite direction, trying to get away from the blue rusted-out truck. A truck that belonged to the same guy who'd punched his nose.

The same guy who would grow up to be a not-so-good guy who drove a truck and drank beer and liked to sometimes hit his wife. A guy Thomas recognized a little too well.

A Special Purpose

Tonight was a good time for Thomas to pray. To thank God that he hadn't gotten beat up today on the side of some unnamed road. And to ask for help for the next week, and next month, and maybe until someone one day handed him his diploma, his get-out-of-jail-free card.

It was dark and quiet. Thomas missed being able to hear the cars passing by on their street back where they used to live. He couldn't rightly call that place home, even though he wasn't sure what else to call it. This place wasn't home either, this barely skinned skeleton surrounding them. Whatever his father's house could be considered, Thomas missed the sounds of life around it. This place was just way too still.

"Dear Jesus, please hear me now."

The youth pastor at their old church taught him to pray. He always said there was not a right or wrong way to pray. Pastor Grady just taught them that they ought to pray all the time. And Thomas did. And he kept believing that it was the right thing to do, that God heard him and cared. Sometimes, especially on nights like this one, Thomas wondered.

"Give me strength, God. Please help me be strong. Help me get through this so that I can do something and make a difference."

This was his prayer.

"Help me make a difference."

This was the prayer of a fifteen-year-old boy.

He had heard Pastor Grady once pray that and he thought it was the coolest thing. This short and balding pastor in a tiny church praying for God to help him make a dent in the world. The guy could've prayed for a bigger church or for more visitors or maybe even for more hair, but instead he'd prayed that he could help the people around him.

That had stuck with Thomas.

Later in life, he might be able to. He liked to dream that he was playing on a pro team and he had young kids looking up at him. That was when he could make a difference, when he could be a positive role model. But now he just needed to figure out how to make it through the day without getting beat up or getting those looks from kids who didn't know or care about him.

You have to stand on solid ground before reaching out to the rest of the world, he thought. And his ground was pretty shaky.

Thomas couldn't pray for more solid ground, however. That felt wrong. He could pray for his mother and his sister and even his father, but he couldn't pray to win the lottery or for a better house or life. That just didn't feel right to him.

So he prayed to make a difference.

"Anybody can change the world," Pastor Grady once said.

It was the sort of thing that politicians said. But Thomas still liked to believe it.

He liked to believe that he was called for a special purpose. And that special purpose didn't have to be twenty years in the future. It might be twenty minutes away. One never knew.

Thomas believed that if he asked, the door would open. If he prayed for something, God would show him if He wanted to answer. It didn't mean He would always answer it, but He might.

One would never know if he didn't ask.

So Thomas dared to ask.

Part of the Plan

"*Do you want* the 'Cookie Doughn't You Want Some' or the 'Ain't Lovin' No Oven'?"

Kevin stood next to the kitchen table where Jenny sat, a stack of mail in front of her, an assortment of bills scattered and organized with the checkbook waiting to get to work. Jenny looked up and appeared surprised by the question and the keys in Kevin's hand. It was eight-thirty at night and they'd just gotten Gregory to sleep.

"Cold Stone Creamery? Now?"

Kevin nodded. "You just said how badly you wanted ice cream."

"That's a bit of a hike."

"I'll get both," he said, smiling.

"Is the game over?"

He shot a glance at the television in the family room, then shook his head.

"The Gamecocks are losing. I've given up on them."

"Or is it because I'm paying bills?"

"Hey. I'm being a good husband and answering my wife's cravings."

"Really? And I just bet you're not going to get anything."

Kevin patted his stomach and noticed that yep, it was still there. It was still a little soft and round for his taste since he hadn't managed to get to the gym for a while. The gym could wait.

And maybe our checkbook could afford to lose the hundred bucks we pay every month to be members.

"I might have to try something out."

Jenny laughed. "I saw you checking out the Coldstone Web site earlier."

"'That's How I Roll.'"

"What?"

"That's what I'm going to get. 'That's How I Roll.' It's got—let's see—cake-batter ice cream, cinnamon, yellow cake, and pecans."

"You and your nuts," Jenny said, taking out a bill and unfolding it.

"You callin' me nuts?"

"Hey—do you know if we paid the four hundred and fifty dollars to Greenville Memorial Hospital?"

"I doubt it."

Jenny had managed the bills for the last few years but recently Kevin had started taking over. And by "taking over," he was really seeing which bills were absolutely necessary to pay and which ones could wait.

Which ones could wait until re-signing the retainer with Silverschone Investments. Which now wasn't going to happen.

"Aren't you paying the medical bills?" Jenny asked, that look of concern clouding her face. "We get a couple a day, it seems."

"I'm just wanting to see which ones our insurance covers."

"You know we don't have maternity coverage."

Kevin opened his mouth and widened his eyes in a mock expression of shock. If someone didn't know him, they might actually buy the look.

"Are you serious?" he asked. "If I'd known that, I would have adopted a puppy instead."

"Stop," Jenny said, rolling her eyes.

"I'm just going to try and get through this year."

"And then what?"

"Then—we'll see. Or I'll see."

There's still time for us to pack up the car and head south. To somewhere far away. Like Key West. Or the Bermuda Triangle.

"This is important, Kev."

"Yes, and so is my question."

She held her belly for a moment. "I'm sore."

"Too sore for ice cream?"

Jenny sighed and looked at the collection of statements in front of her. "I guess not."

"Let me go get some ice cream, and when I get back I'll do these and you can relax. Okay?"

"I can work on these while you're gone."

He put his hands on her shoulders. "You don't have to. It just stresses you out."

"It stresses you out too," Jenny said. "You just ignore it."

I don't ignore. I bury.

"No I don't. Listen, we've talked about this."

"I'd hate to add this all up. Our Visa bill came in. It's almost up to twenty thousand."

"That's good news," Kevin said. "It's a nice round number we can remember. Plus, think of the points we're getting."

"This isn't funny."

"It's going to be fine, Jen."

"Says who?"

"It will. Trust me."

She gave him a look that didn't resemble any form of trust. Instead it resembled a shade of skepticism crossed with worry.

I used to have her trust. I used to have her belief.

He used to also trust that God played a part in this. He could have said, "Trust God," but he didn't. That would have been hypocritical.

It's great to say "Have faith in one another and in God" when you have steady income.

"Maybe I should go back to work," Jen said.

"Jen, please, no." He sat down in the chair next to her. He'd hoped to get out, to get her some ice cream and not go this direction. But it was inevitable. "Come on. How are you going to do that?"

"People do it all the time."

"No. We already have our hands full with Gregory. Two more boys won't be enough?"

"My mom can help."

The worst part of conversations like this was that he couldn't give Jenny a definitive answer. He couldn't say, "We're going to land some new jobs and survive another six months." He didn't know if Precision Design could survive another six weeks. He was taking it a day at a time. If he suddenly started thinking about every potential bill coming in—especially the hospital bills that were approaching with the delivery costs, which were all out of pocket—he might go crazy. Or feel completely out of control.

Kevin leaned over and took her hands in his.

"Just don't worry about these, okay?" Kevin said in a calm tone that was as much for himself as for Jenny.

"Somebody has to."

Ouch.

"Jen—"

She glanced at the checkbook, then closed it.

"Ain't Lovin' No Oven.' Might as well eat my way to the poorhouse if that's where we're headed."

He laughed. "See—that's the spirit."

"Just hurry home so it doesn't totally melt."

"Yes, sir," he said as he stood at attention and gave her a salute.

*

The imagined conversation in bed went something like this:

"Jen?"

"Yeah?"

They would have been speaking in darkness, the only light the alarm clock showing the time as 1:14 A.M.

"It's going to be okay," he would have said, an arm around her side and a gentle hand on her stomach.

"I'm worried." Her voice would be soft and weighted in the darkness.

"I know. But God's going to take care of things. He'll take care of us."

This was his alternate self talking in their alternate universe. The nice kind that resided a few towns away from Pleasantville.

"That doesn't mean we shouldn't be responsible," Jenny could have said.

"We just need to pray. Why don't we pray together?"

And then in the echoes of his imagination, Kevin would pray, holding Jen's hand, waiting for her to pray too.

Instead, Kevin heard her slow, steady breathing. She was out. Full from eating every drop of ice cream and tired from the two growing boys inside of her. She slept light as a mouse but also got tired early and stayed tired.

Praying together in the middle of the night was a nice thing that some couples might do. And something that one day they might do. All he knew now was that they had never been a praying couple. And lately, Kevin hadn't been much for praying altogether.

Somewhere in the journey of trying to be a leader at his firm and in his industry, Kevin forgot to be a leader at home. A leader who guided them financially, emotionally, even spiritually.

Spiritually? Yeah, right.

Faith was one thing, but action was another. Faith was this mysterious, strange entity that he couldn't fully understand or grab hold of. Business and life and money were all things that lay in his control.

Nothing's in your control, Kevin, and you of all people should know that.

When it was just him in the middle of the night, without the busyness of the day knocking on his door or the sounds of family or colleagues or friends surrounding him, Kevin would wade into this deep end of worry. It remained there like a pool in the backyard that was never emptied or cleaned. It grew dark and murky yet he just stared at it, taking no action.

Soon there would be no choice *but* to take action. Soon he'd be dealing with closing shop, right around the time the twins arrived.

Hello, I'm your father, and I just declared bankruptcy! Nice to meet ya both!

Another voice reminded Kevin that Jenny and he had wanted these babies desperately—that they had prayed to have more children. Well, Jenny especially.

Turning on his side in bed, facing the orange dial on the clock that seemed to mock him, Kevin knew that this—all of this—was a gigantic answer to prayer. There had been the time when he had complained about being a corporate slave when he really wanted to run his own firm. There was also the time he was angry and resentful that they weren't having luck trying to start a family.

These were blessings in his life: the fact that he was running his own business and the wonderful fact that their family was about to grow.

I just want a little breathing room.

But that had never been part of the deal, part of the plan, part of the prayer. Kevin knew this too. Kevin knew that life wasn't easy. Even for those who might appear to have it easy, he knew that nobody had a perfect life. Money or fame or security didn't assure anyone of anything.

His mind drifted and he realized just how little he'd changed over the years. He should be able to stand firmly alongside Jenny and tell her not to worry. He should be able to stand firmly alongside God and know he didn't *need* to worry. Both of their parents had that steadfast faith that people talked about and that he always assumed he'd have one day when he grew up.

But he was still a kid, whose biggest decision was what ice cream flavor to pick at the end of another endless day.

Maybe it was finally time for Kevin to grow up.

Generosity

"Mom?"

For a second Lynn thought she was dreaming. She thought she was in the same bed with Daryl, and four-year-old Thomas was whispering to her and the promise of a better tomorrow woke up beside her.

"Mom, wake up."

When she opened her eyes, that four-year-old boy was nearly a man. He stood at the side of her bed, the light from the cracks in the old blinds streaming into the small room. She sat up, instantly worried.

"There's something wrong with the toilet."

"What?"

Okay, it's not Sara.

"It's like—I don't know. You just gotta take a look at it."

She rubbed her forehead and yawned. She felt like she could sleep until noon on this rare Sunday morning she had off. Work had been particularly busy last night, but it had also been particularly rewarding with a couple of really nice tips. She'd gone to bed in a hopeful mood and she hadn't wanted it to end.

She followed Thomas out the room and a few steps to the open doorway. Sara stood in there looking like she was gagging on something. The floor around the toilet was wet. She heard strange clanging noises.

"What happened?" Lynn asked.

"Nothing," Sara said. "I heard some weird noises and came in and it started overflowing."

Lynn watched the toilet for a few seconds. Nothing.

"Are you sure?"

"Yes!"

Still nothing happened.

She was about ready to get something to clean up the floor of the bathroom when a fountain sprayed straight up from the toilet. Sara squealed with laughter and Thomas was smiling, pointing at it to prove his point.

"Something's wrong," he said.

"Really?" She nudged him with her arm.

The toilet suddenly seemed to inhale, not flush, sucking all its water down. Then it gurgled and began to fill again. The sounds of pipes straining came again.

"I better tell Mr. Sinclair."

"It stinks," Sara said.

"It could be worse," Thomas told her.

A gush of water sprayed up again from the toilet, making both Lynn and Sara jolt from surprise. This caused them all to start laughing even more. Lynn moved next to the toilet and turned the knob until the water stopped spurting.

"Hope neither of you need to use the restroom this morning," Lynn said.

As she walked into the living area and toward the kitchen, she thought of last night. One of the customers who'd come in had been very generous. Of course, he'd watched her like a hawk. Perhaps there'd been more to that tip than simple customer satisfaction. But Lynn gladly took it.

"Hey guys," she said to them as she looked at a bare cupboard. "Want to go out for breakfast?"

Sara screamed in excitement and Thomas asked where.

"How about that family restaurant on the way to school? We can stop by the Sinclairs' and let them know about the toilet."

"You sure?" Thomas asked.

Lynn nodded, understanding his question. "Yeah."

"Let's go!" Sara was already heading outside.

"Well, let your mother get dressed first, okay?"

*

It was nice to be out, to be with the kids and ordering from a menu and letting someone else cook for them. Granny's was only open for breakfast and lunch. They were known for their pancakes and their bakery. Lynn and the kids had never come here since moving, even though they'd passed it by almost daily. It took them a few minutes to get a table.

Lynn remembered those early days after first moving to Georgia when they would go to breakfast after church on Sundays. Thomas was four and Sara was just a baby and Daryl didn't work on the weekends at the factory. She could still picture her husband ordering the biggest meal they had and wolfing it down like some kind of lumberjack. They'd stay for a while, Daryl drinking coffee and talking more with each cup.

The good old days.

She never would have imagined that so many years later, it would just be the three of them.

Since moving, they had only made it to church a few times. She worked most Sunday mornings. That was the reason she gave the kids for not going. She wasn't sure if now was the best time to start going to a church, especially since they hadn't done a great job of that back home. Except for Thomas, of course.

Inside Granny's, the kids joked about the possessed toilet until they started getting crude and Lynn was forced to change the subject. Thomas ordered a pecan waffle with bacon while Sara got chocolate-chip pancakes that came out looking more like a sundae than breakfast.

Talk turned to Christmas and Thomas asked a question that Lynn had asked herself several times.

"Are we really going to get those Christmas presents we asked for?"

Lynn finished the bite of her omelet. "I'm sure you will. I'm heading to the Salvation Army today to give them your lists. Then I'll have to go there a few days before Christmas to pick them up."

"You don't have to do anything to get them?" Thomas asked. "Like trade in Sara for them?"

"Ha ha," Sara said.

"They've been doing this for years. That's what the woman I spoke to on the phone at the Salvation Army said. She said they've got it down to a science. It's very organized. I just bring my identification and everything else should be taken care of."

"Is Dad sending us presents?"

"No," Thomas said to Sara in an annoyed voice. He reached over with his fork and took a bite of her pancake.

"Stop."

"You can have some of mine."

"I don't like pecans."

"Picky."

"Sweetie, your father doesn't know where we are," Lynn reminded Sara.

"Like, forever?"

"Don't talk with your mouth full," Lynn said. "Not forever. Just at the moment."

I'm taking it a day at a time, sweetie, so I can't speak for forever

"So we're not going to get Christmas presents from Dad for the second year in a row?" Sara said.

Lynn glanced at her daughter. She loved her little girl to death but sometimes she hated that selfish and whiny tone. Sara wasn't always like that. But sometimes she just couldn't help herself.

"We need to be thankful for what we have," Lynn said. "Like the nice tip last night that allowed us to go out."

"I'm thankful for the bathrooms at this place," Thomas said.

They laughed again, and Sara started talking about the water shooting up from the toilet bowl. It was amazing how bathroom humor never seemed to get old when you were a kid.

As they finished their meal and the bill came, Lynn thought about the tip. Then she realized that there was no way she couldn't be generous, not after last night. She shuffled through the singles in her wallet and pulled aside ten of them for the server, a young woman probably in her twenties.

Maybe generosity can be contagious.

Lynn hoped that it might be.

On the way out the door, they passed a small, decorated Christmas tree with presents underneath. She doubted that Mr. Sinclair had gotten a chance to come by the trailer to fix the toilet.

"Hey guys—I've got an idea," she told them. "Want to go find a Christmas tree?"

Getting Worse

Mom's Nissan wasn't just beat up. Rust was eating away at the paint on the back. Its frame was bent, so it drove as if it was sliding sideways. Its engine sounded like an old man's cough, the kind that came from smoking for sixty years. Half the time, whenever Mom accelerated, it would jerk and burp and then rumble as if it was contemplating dying. So far it hadn't totally died, but it was going to. When it did, they wouldn't be able to take it in to a shop like most families. Other families struggling with bad cars had credit cards to buy them a little time until they could get all the money for repairs, but Thomas's family didn't.

This was one reason Thomas took the school bus, even though he hated it. It was a choice between a long bus ride or a short but uncertain car ride. But on this Monday morning, since he'd overslept and nobody had woken him up, Thomas had to either skip school or be driven there by his mother. And he had already gotten in trouble once for skipping school when this happened, so he couldn't do it again.

"You didn't wake me up."

"You have an alarm by your bed," Mom said.

"It went off when the power went out sometime last night."

"I heard your sister calling you."

"I ignore her when she calls my name," Thomas said, tying the frayed laces on his basketball shoes. "She's usually complaining about something."

"Are you ready to go?" Mom looked on the kitchen counter for the car keys.

Thomas scratched his head. "I'll never be ready to go back to school."

"That bad?"

"It ain't good."

Mom looked like she was going to say something but she stopped herself. He grabbed the backpack and went to the car. The beast.

Maybe there wouldn't be many kids noticing him being dropped off. Maybe he could even figure out a way to get his mother to drop him off before they reached school.

*

On the way, Thomas noticed something new about the car.

It now roared . . . but not in a good way.

The engine made a racket that Thomas was sure echoed for miles and miles.

"When did the muffler go?"

"It's been gone a few weeks."

He hadn't noticed it, not even when they went to get breakfast on Sunday morning.

Now there was no way he could go unnoticed driving up to school.

Surely she can drop me off a few blocks before the school, right?

But he couldn't bring himself to ask.

So when the car pulled up in the busy parking lot of the busy high school, Thomas wanted to wear a bag over his head. Half the students around him didn't care, but it didn't matter because the other half of them noticed and stared.

This was the part of the whole experience of being a new kid he hated. Being noticed. Being studied and scrutinized. Being judged. Because he had a pretty good idea what kind of picture the other kids were drawing in their heads when it came to Thomas Brandt.

"Have a good day," Mom said.

"Thanks."

He climbed out and shut the door and began to walk, expecting to hear the loud blast of engine behind him.

Instead, he didn't hear anything.

He turned and looked at the old car.

It had stalled.

Now he was hearing a whirring sound as his mom kept turning the key in the ignition without success.

You've gotta be kidding.

For a brief moment he thought about bailing. He would never have done it but the thought did go through his mind.

Thomas walked back over to the car and opened the passenger door.

"It died on me."

"So I hear."

"It's not my fault."

The anger and awkwardness inside of him wanted to say something, but Mom was right. It wasn't her fault.

A car behind them honked. Thomas waved them past and the car bolted around them, its driver looking angry.

"We better move this," Thomas said.

"How?"

"Here, just—put it in neutral and I'll try to push it. Let's try to roll it to the parking lot. Or at least away from the sidewalk."

A group of girls gawked as they passed by. He didn't want them noticing him. Not his mom's car or his familiar jeans or his very worn T-shirt or anything about him.

Another thought sank like a torpedo in his mind.

Was that Cass?

But no. He didn't want to think about that because he was pretty sure she was somewhere out there watching him, now when he was all red-faced from not only trying to move a car too heavy for one kid but also blushing from the tip of his nose to the bottom of his toes.

He heaved with all his strength but the car wouldn't budge.

"You have it in neutral? Is the brake off?"

"Yeah."

Another car honked.

A group of students walked by laughing. Maybe at him, maybe not.

Then he heard a voice shouting from a distance. "Need a new car, buddy?"

He didn't have to look to see that it was Vic. Thomas searched the sidewalk and saw him standing with a group of friends, all of them laughing. Vic towered over the rest of them with his tall frame and his spiked hair.

"Want to borrow mine?"

"I can get out," Mom said.

"No, Mom, you need to steer."

This was getting worse. More kids were staring, more cars were behind them waiting.

Someone tapped his shoulder.

For a brief moment Thomas thought of punching whoever it was. Surely it was someone needing this space, someone who was impatient and thought they were far more important than the rest of the world, someone who didn't understand.

But instead he saw the round face of a guy he'd seen but had never met. He was smiling.

"Need some help?" the guy asked.

"Yeah, sure, thanks."

The guy was big—he played football. Thomas had seen him walking around with the rest of the football team. This guy definitely had to be a lineman, probably offensive tackle or something like that. The stranger called out to a couple other guys and they all pushed the Maxima with ease. They made jokes while they did it, but with each other, not with him.

With each foot they moved, Thomas felt relieved. They moved the car to an empty parking spot away from the drop-off portion of the lot.

"Thanks."

"Yeah, sure," the stranger said. "I can get my truck to try and jump it."

"Are you sure? Will you be late for class?"

"Aw, it's fine. Just stay here. Teacher won't mind me helpin' someone out."

"Okay."

As the big guy moved slowly to go back to the parking lot, someone called out his name.

"Carlos, where're you going?"

Thomas thought for a moment.

Carlos.

Carlos was surely not a Vic.

It was nice to know that not everybody at the school made outsiders feel like outsiders.

Bah Humbug

As he climbed out of his car, the early morning cold woke Kevin up to the chilling reality he faced.

For a moment he wanted a big snow. A major kind that would shut down the city for a week. Then maybe he could think. Then maybe he could make sense of everything.

He thought of something his father once told him. "There's a fine line between getting ahead and getting ahead of ourselves."

Kevin wasn't sure exactly where that fine line was, but as he stood by his car staring at the building in front of him, he worried that he had passed over the line some time ago.

The handsome brick building was only a few years old. The loft on the third floor belonged to him, to Precision Design. All 1,500 square feet. So did the lease that he had just renewed.

Up in smoke. Poof. Just like that.

He could remember wanting to create ever since he began to store memories in his life's well. His parents had encouraged him in his drawing, though he learned early on that he wasn't excited about art itself. Painting for the sake of painting didn't inspire him. Photography intrigued him more, and for a long time he had aspirations of being some kind of famous photographer. Maybe someone like Annie Leibovitz, who took shots of famous people for magazines like *Vanity Fair.* Or maybe someone like Anton Corbijn, who was famous for his photos of bands like U2. But through college, Kevin learned that the direction he wanted to go—the direction that actually could earn him a living—would be in marketing and advertising.

Early in his career at a publishing house, he learned that it was one thing to get a paycheck and benefits and climb the corporate ladder. But that drained him. Nothing about it inspired him. He wanted the freedom to do what he loved and he knew that he had the ability to do it like some of the other big players. Kevin just needed a big break.

That big break came in the form of a friendship.

It's not what you know but who you know. So they say.

Though Kevin didn't necessarily believe that, he did agree that in this case, it was *exactly* who he knew.

The campaign that had paved the way for this building and this business was forged by a friendship with a man he'd worked with briefly who ended up going to another company.

That man was Dan Harris. That friendship and business relationship had allowed him to pursue his dreams.

He sighed, then headed into the office.

*

Every Monday morning at Precision Design, everybody would meet in the conference room at nine o'clock. This was one of Kevin's favorite parts of the week—to get everybody together, see how their weekend went, share some stories, laugh a lot, and then talk about the upcoming week. It was a meeting that he'd held for a few years now, and it still didn't feel routine or forced. He enjoyed the way everybody strolled in at a leisurely pace, bringing a cup of coffee and a notebook or their laptops to take notes on.

This Monday was the first day back since the meeting in New York. And because of who he was and the company he'd built, Kevin wasn't about to keep that information from them.

I'm going to tell them everything I can.

He took a sip of his coffee and glanced around the conference room. This was a great snapshot of Precision, with its modern black-and-white furniture and sleek layout. Awards littered the wall in a decorative rather than ostentatious way. Small pieces of the ten-year history of the company could be seen everywhere, from the groundhog that had been the star of an early campaign for a golf resort to the signed picture of James Gandolfini, who'd been involved in a charity that Precision helped worked with.

In the silence before the rest of the gang arrived, Kevin thought about what he was going to say, but then he shoved those thoughts away. This didn't require any sort of rehearsed speech. He was going to just be honest and straightforward. That was how he approached all of his clients and employees. He hated playing games, stalling, running around the obvious. The team deserved to know what had happened with Silverschone Investments.

Zack Shields came in first, as usual. He was probably the most talented person on his team, and Kevin was including himself in that roster. Zack was an insanely creative designer and he could do things with a speed that astounded Kevin. Zack's only negative was his age. At twenty-five, he still needed to learn the art of taking input and satisfying customers' needs. Sometimes Zack could do something that visually was a masterpiece, yet it didn't match what the client had originally asked for.

"Morning," Zack said as he sat down in one of the comfortable armchairs and put his iPad on the table.

They won't be getting a Christmas present like that this year.

Last year, after a nice profitable year, Kevin had surprised everybody at Precision with a new iPad. He could justify giving them out because it did *help* with their jobs. It wasn't crucial, but happy employees were motivated employees. Zack especially had flipped after receiving the gift.

"Did you see it yet?" Zack asked, his eyebrows raising behind stylish, square glasses. Kevin wondered whether they were plain glass or actually prescription.

The young designer started talking about the latest Apple announcement that Kevin had somehow missed. As he did, Jamie Lang came in. Jamie was Kevin's studio manager, who stayed on top of everybody's projects and made sure Kevin was able to successfully run Precision without having to hold everybody's hand. She carried her trusty file folders, which kept her organized and kept everybody else on task and moving forward. Kevin didn't care how somebody went about doing their job as long as they did it, and Jamie had been doing her job very well for the last four years.

The rest of the team came in at once. Samantha, a newer designer who Kevin joked about being so quiet he was nervous that she was hiding some deep, dark secret from them all. Then there was Pete Dawson, an all-around good guy who loved beer and the Braves. He had a cool vibe about him that he somehow managed to weave into his work. Many times Pete touched up little parts of everybody's projects, making them better. Pete was all about the fine details, which ultimately meant making the company look better.

"Y'all are going to love to hear about my weekend," Beth Anne said as she walked in.

It was hard for anybody not to love the demonstrative southern charm of Beth Anne, who had grown up in Greenville and spent a year working in New York only to come back to her beloved city. Beth Anne was Kevin's accounts manager, the liaison between the designers and all of their clients. She spent a lot of time on the phone, updating customers on the status of their projects and checking in with others. If anybody had a reason to be worried this morning, it was Beth Anne. She knew how important Kevin's meeting with Silverschone had been, but if she held any worry, it certainly didn't show.

Mia Chen walked with a quiet and slow grace, gliding in and sitting in the last chair around the table. For a while they talked as they usually did, laughing, listening to Beth Anne's funny but tragic tale about a double date she'd gone on with her sister.

Kevin thought of all the people around him in this conference room, taking inventory of them in a way he hadn't done in a long time or maybe even ever.

These are lives I'm responsible for. People that I have to answer to.

He didn't want to finish the thought, the one about letting them down. Because Precision wasn't done just yet. Almost, but not quite.

"All right, so . . ." Kevin eventually said, breaking into the conversation that could go for another hour. "I'm going to change pace a little this morning and start with some news."

"Should we be worried?" Beth Anne asked in the same comical tone that she'd used in relaying the dating story.

"No. But—well . . ."

Beth Anne didn't respond this time.

I was as surprised as you, Kevin thought. *I didn't see this coming, not ever.*

Six faces that he knew and loved looked at him.

Jamie and Mia were the only two employees who were married. Jamie had a couple of kids. Both had husbands who worked. There wasn't one sole and solitary breadwinner who was in danger of losing their job.

If they indeed do end up losing their jobs.

But it didn't matter. Every single one of his employees had gotten the big dream speech when they first applied and when he finally hired them. The dream of working in an environment where people cared about one another and had fun and delivered exceptional service. A place of people who created because they loved to create. A place that was a business, but really at heart they were in the business of making magic happen, of designing a form around an idea, about creating something from nothing.

"So I had this idea last night that I wanted us all to meet outside in a field."

"It's kind of cold for baseball," Pete joked.

"Well, I thought of it—no. I was going to give each of you a bat, then unveil Hal sitting in the center of the field. I was going to let you all enact our favorite scene from *Office Space*."

"We still have time," Jamie said as she stood up, acting like she was ready to go.

Jamie naturally would have been the one out of all of them to love his suggestion. She was the one who worked the most with the old Power Mac G5 that Kevin bought half a decade ago. It was at a desk that some of the interns used. The only reason Kevin still kept it was for all the old files on it. They'd nicknamed this problematic computer "Hal" from the legendary computer that went psychotic in *2001*.

"You think I'm joking," Kevin said. "But you all might want to after hearing about my trip."

"That's doesn't sound very promising," Beth Anne said. She shook her head, knowing him probably too well. "You're worrying me."

"Okay, so as you know, day before Thanksgiving, I met with Silverschone. And well, unfortunately they didn't want to sign another retainer for the coming year."

The energy and excitement was suddenly sucked from the room, like a balloon instantly deflating. Kevin saw their reactions, but he kept on talking.

"I know I told all of you when you first came to work here that we were going to do something great. I think we have. And I think we're going to continue to do some good things. I hope. But you know how it goes—I don't like companies that aren't straight up with us. I gotta be the same way." He paused and took a deep breath before he said what he knew he had to: "I can't promise you that Precision will make it to the end of the year."

"Serious?" Pete said with a look of total disbelief.

Half of them looked as devastated as if they'd just watched him get beaten up. The other half looked like they weren't hearing his words correctly.

"You all know how much work we do for Silverschone," Kevin said. "And there was always this possibility—"

"Why?" Beth Anne asked, her need to fix things obvious in the question.

"You can guess the why—the economy, cutbacks, their company."

"Is there anything we could have done?"

Kevin shook his head and smiled at Beth Anne. "No. Every one of you—and I mean this—has done an extraordinary job. I mean that."

He could practically hear the sound of six plane engines roaring to life, thoughts racing in their heads, wondering what they were going to do and what was next.

"I wanted all of you to know right away because—because I want to give you time in case something doesn't come in by the first of the year. It doesn't mean I'm giving up—that we should give up. There's a lot that we can still do."

"Like what?" Pete asked.

"We still have some projects—some money waiting to come in, some potential clients. I know going into December and Christmas—this is pretty much the worst kind of news I could possibly give you. And I want you to know that I'm going to try to do everything I can to keep this company alive."

"What can we do?" Zack asked.

"Look, before everybody goes crazy and starts trying every possible lead they can, I want all of you to hear this: every one of you has an amazing talent that—if forced to go somewhere else—I know you will continue to do incredible work." Kevin carefully made sure to look at every one of them in the eyes as he spoke. "I want you to know that I'll do anything I can to help you find something else if Precision ends up shutting its doors."

"Just like that? I mean, you would close your doors just like that?"

Pete seemed dumbfounded. Beth Anne and Jamie weren't as completely blown away. They knew more than the designers how close to the edge Precision had been for some time.

I was close when I went on my own. Then I got even closer when I began hiring. Then I really neared the edge when I leased these offices.

With this latest obstacle, the stretch marks were really starting to show, and no amount of cocoa butter was going to prevent that.

"Kev—I'm so sorry," Beth Anne said, looking like he just told them that a family member had died.

"Beth Anne, thank you. But look, we're not shut down yet. Who knows what can happen in one month?"

"You're gonna have twins, that's what can happen."

"Guys, it's just—stop," Kevin said, noting the deathly expressions on their faces. "I think things will be fine. There's just one thing . . ."

The glance he gave everybody was equally serious. No hint of any kind of humor could be detected. They waited for him to continue.

"I hate to do this," Kevin said. "But I'm going to need to ask for you to give me back your iPads. I'm really sorry."

Zack opened his mouth slightly, aghast. "Are you serious?" The rest of the gang laughed as Zack held on to the iPad for dear life.

Kevin shook his head. "No. I'm sorry—that probably wasn't very funny." He grinned.

It was good to see that they could still laugh. Sometimes, that was all one could do.

This was probably what he'd miss most. Not all the money they made or all the projects they created, but ultimately the relationships around this table. They mattered.

It was nice to be reminded of that.

*

"How'd it go today?"

They walked slowly on the sidewalk alongside the outdoor mall. It was Jenny's choice to come here even though Kevin had said they didn't need to go shopping. She wanted the exercise, reminding him that she wasn't bedridden and still had a lot of Christmas gifts to get including his. Kevin didn't want to tell her how unsuccessful he'd been at finding a gift for her the day after Thanksgiving, but he figured he might be able to make a little progress this evening.

He shrugged at his wife's question. "Pretty good. Only a couple burst into tears. Another couple quit immediately."

Unlike Zack, Jenny knew when he was teasing. She gave him a mild smile in response, meaning she wanted a serious answer.

"They took it fine," he said. "Better than I thought."

"What'd you say?"

"I told them everything I know. Nothing is final just yet."

"It will be pretty soon."

He nodded, waited as a few teens strolled between them, then looked back at her. "Maybe something miraculous will happen this month."

"Like what?"

"Well, I was hoping you'd pull a *It's a Wonderful Life* for me and go around to all our friends and relatives to collect cash."

Jenny chuckled at this. "You planning on going to jail?"

"Do you need me to?"

"Well, if you're going to, try and make it *after* the twins come."

"February, then?"

She shook her head and raised her eyebrows. "That might be a little too ambitious."

"Why?"

"I'm thinking I won't make it to February."

"We're taking it a day at a time. That's what I told everybody at work too. That's all we can do."

They walked up to the sporting-goods store. Jenny wanted to look for some gifts for her side of the family and maybe even for him. "Do they have motivation bottled in a can to get me to work out?" he joked with her before heading inside. He knew that she was anxious to start working out as soon as she could after the twins were born, a nice idea in theory. Still it didn't mean Kevin couldn't give her motivation by getting her new workout clothes or perhaps some new shoes.

When they walked into the store, the first thing he saw was a Christmas tree front and center in the store.

It's following me. The tree. It's haunting me.

Upon studying it, Kevin realized that it was quite different from the tree he'd spotted at the mall. It wasn't as large and didn't have as many paper angels decorating it. But it was still the same kind of tree—one of those Angel Trees that he'd managed to escape.

He almost managed to do the same thing this time. But instead, he felt the tug of Jenny's hand at his coat.

"Look, Kev."

"Yeah, I see," he said.

What he meant was *Yeah, I've seen it before, now can we just move on?*

"We should pick two ornaments off the tree."

He stopped in front of the tree, wondering if he'd heard his wife correctly.

"Don't give me that look," she said.

"What look?"

"That look. It's a good idea. We each pick one."

Of course it's a good idea. And a lot of people pick ornaments because it's a good thing to do. But people like me don't because you know—

Jenny didn't wait for him but instead moved and picked an ornament from the bottom of the tree. "Steph."

Kevin was still frozen. He hated being forced to do something, and he didn't want to have to buy things for someone he didn't know and would never know and wanted God knew what—

"Kev," Jenny said in a get-on-with-it tone.

"Okay, fine."

"Nice holiday spirit," she teased.

He did the opposite of what she did, picking a paper ornament from the top.

See, already I'm doing this kid a huge favor. Aren't I a saint?

"See how difficult that was?" Jenny asked. "So much hard work."

"If this kid wants a flat screen TV, he isn't getting it."

"I'm going to call you Scrooge."

"Hey," Kevin said as they walked past the tree toward the men's clothing section. "Scrooge was single. Remember that."

"So?"

"So what?" He didn't want to get into it, not here in the store.

She's wanting to do something nice even though I'm worried how we're going to pay any of our bills next month.

"Who'd you get?" Jenny asked. "Are you even going to look at the ornament?"

"I was hoping you'd look away and I could slide it back onto the tree. Being Scrooge and all."

Jenny swiped the ornament from his hand.

"Thomas."

"That's his name?" Kevin asked.

"Yes. Fifteen years old. Clothing is size large. Shoes size eleven. Wants Nike basketball shoes. An iPod. A digital camera. And a Michael Jordan Bulls jersey."

"Shut up."

"Serious."

Kevin couldn't tell if Jenny was kidding. "Let me see that."

Sure enough, a Michael Jordan jersey was on the list.

"Oh man," he said in a bit of disbelief. "Is this all? I don't even want to see your list."

"Bah humbug," Jenny said as she puckered up her lips in a mock grouchy look.

"Even when you try you can't look mean."

"Don't test me."

Kevin folded the paper ornament and slipped it into his coat pocket. He quickly forgot about it as he shopped for his wife. It was only later after he got home that he found the name and the list and realized that he had already failed miserably. He could have easily gotten the basketball shoes at the sporting-goods store, yet he hadn't.

He had a lot to learn about the art of giving back.

Thin and Shredded

Being new was like wearing a dirty old coat to school every day—and there wasn't a thing he could do to change it. Thomas wondered when he could finally take it off and breathe a little easier. But almost a year since arriving at Greer High and that old coat still clung to him. Kids didn't really bother noticing him because they already had their friends. He didn't fit into a box and he didn't look interesting or rich or funny or peculiar enough to make others take note. Thomas just looked like an old coat you ignored in a closet day after day.

The only people who actually did notice him were the ones he wanted to leave him alone.

People like Vic, who had suddenly found his mission in life: annoy Thomas as much as he possibly could.

Bullies don't just beat you up. They badger and belittle and break down every single good thing until you are broken. Thomas knew that the ground he walked on was cracking ice. It was just a matter of time before he was going to plunge into the freezing depths below.

Today might be the day.

It started with the bus and the silent stares and the small bubble of isolation surrounding him. Nobody ever bothered to talk to him or even say hi. A girl on the bus named Naomi stumbled on his backpack. She gave him a look like she was smelling something really bad, and it was coming from him.

Vic got to him before his first class. The guy's locker was on the other side of the school but he'd managed to make a special trip just to see Thomas.

"What's up, champ?" Vic said.

Thomas nodded as he took out some of the books in his locker.

"Next time we'll catch you."

He of course was referring to the game of tag they'd played. Thomas on foot and Vic in his truck.

"Gonna be quiet, huh?"

Vic wore a faded Metallica T-shirt, old and dirty jeans, and shoes that looked almost shabbier that the ones Thomas wore. He had the slightest bit of facial hair on his face in bits and pieces. Thomas really wanted to say something about the hilarious look Vic had going on, but he bit his tongue.

"You think this is a purdy big high school, don't you?" His accent was thick today.

I'm not sure what purdy *means, you dumb redneck.*

"You can't get away from me," Vic continued. "You're gonna be seeing a lot of me."

This was a nice way to start the day. Yesterday, their car broke down. Now this.

Next came second period, where the two of them shared the same English class. Thomas doubted that Vic was ever going to be a Shakespeare or even James Patterson—he paid too little attention and made too little effort. Usually, Vic tried to draw embarrassing attention to Thomas. Sometimes he would just be outright mean, calling across the room—before the teacher came in—names like "trailer trash" or "hillbilly." Sometimes he would follow Thomas after class, harassing him and pushing to get into a fight. The worst came earlier today when Vic decided to engage others in the game.

"Where'd you get that T-shirt, zitface? Hey, Tank, you ever heard of this brand?"

Stuff like this.

"You know they got stuff out today that can help you with acne?" Vic said about the pimples on Thomas's chin.

Every single thing Vic could think of belittling him for, he did. Mrs. Hayne told him numerous times to stop talking in the back of the room, but she obviously had no idea what he was talking about.

Thomas would have told anybody who asked that the taunts and the names meant nothing. But they stung. They peeled away layers of self-confidence, and word after word and encounter after encounter left him feeling thin and shredded.

In the last class before the end of the day, as kids spoke about upcoming Christmas vacations and what they wanted for the holiday, Thomas could only think of one thing.

It wasn't the list that he'd given to his mom for the Angel Tree. He seriously doubted he was going to get any of those gifts.

No, Thomas only wanted one gift. To be left alone by Vic, the same way everybody else left him alone.

Opportunities

When the truck pulled up, a part of her seized up while another part of her already starting planning the escape route. All in less than a second as she glanced outside at the white truck.

Then Lynn saw a stranger approaching and realized it wasn't him.

Daryl hadn't finally decided to show up at her front door and try to bring them all back home.

Yet.

It had almost been a year, and the only interaction with her husband had been the few times she'd called and then hung up on him from a phone at the restaurant before saying anything. Daryl didn't have caller ID, but he probably knew it was her. She wasn't quite sure why she'd called.

Maybe to check and see if he was still alive.

He probably assumed she'd come back to the Greer area since some of her family still lived out there. She wondered if Daryl had called her sister and brother, but neither of them knew she had moved back. Not that they would have been overjoyed anyway. Daryl had been the one who promised her years ago when they first married that he was rescuing Lynn from her drug-taking white-trash family.

As the door on the trailer rattled from the knocks, Lynn held a hand over her heart and breathed in for a moment. It would probably take a half hour to slow down.

"Can I help you?" she asked the man at her door.

"You called about your stove."

She had been so scared she had forgotten that Mr. Sinclair had gotten someone to come in to see about the stove. "Oh, yes, please come in."

A part of her wanted to double-check and see if her husband was anywhere around, but she forced herself to let it go.

An hour later, as the repairman put his tools away and washed his hands, Lynn could see the look on his face as he surveyed the small trailer. It was sad when stove repairman looked with pity at the place where she and her kids lived.

Sometimes life forces you into places you don't want to be.

Lynn was realizing that every day.

"That should do it," the man said.

She thanked him and hoped that no more repairmen would have to enter this house, at least not for another few months. She didn't want Mr. Sinclair to change his mind about letting them stay in this run-down trailer. She had told him they wouldn't be any problem, yet it seemed like she was constantly going over to his house to complain about something else.

As she watched the man start to head out the door, Lynn saw him pause and glance at her living room.

Does he have to keep judging me like this? Go on and get back home to your nice little house with the 2.5 bathrooms and the pretty backyard.

"Excuse me for asking, ma'am, but do y'all have a Christmas tree?"

She was going to say it was none of his business, but the manner in which he asked was friendly enough. "No, we haven't gotten one just yet."

We found some decent ones until I realized how expensive they were.

He nodded, thought for a moment. "You know—I got a Christmas tree in the back of my truck."

"Oh, no, it's fine, thanks. We'll probably find one at the last minute."

This wasn't really true because she doubted they'd go looking for one again after the disappointment the first time.

"Well, what I meant is y'all can have it if you want it. My wife—she's kinda particular about things and she didn't like it. Not that it's a bad tree. I mean—I don't want you thinkin' I'm giving you a bad tree. It's a really good tree but she wanted a bigger one. I don't even know if the place is gonna take it back. You can take a look at it if you want."

Lynn didn't see this coming.

He wants to give me a tree. That's why he was looking at me like that. That's why he was checking out my place and my living room.

She wanted to apologize for thinking poorly of him.

"Yeah, sure," she said. "Thank you."

A voice whispered in her ear as she followed the man to his truck.

Sometimes you don't even have to ask for help, Lynn. Sometimes it's there right in front of your eyes.

She thought about that Christmas dinner at the soup kitchen again. She kept telling herself that they didn't need to go, that the Angel Tree had been a onetime thing before things got better, that she could do it on her own.

But nobody can do it on their own. You know this but deep down you're running.

Maybe Daryl wasn't the only person she was running from.

*

Lady Antebellum blasted, and Sara sang along in front of the mirror into the hairbrush in her hand. Lynn's daughter didn't know she was being watched, but she probably wouldn't have minded if she had known. The song was coming from the tiny radio that she'd bought at a dollar store, and while it didn't have the best sound, the pink AM/FM radio certainly had the best spirit.

It was an adorable sight that filled Lynn with both delight and despair.

The kinky blond hair and swaying hips and feisty spirit could have been her twenty-some years ago when she was that age, singing to the sweet sounds of Patty Loveless.

"Mom!" Sara looked at her, her hands on her hips.

"Don't stop for me." She walked into the tiny room and slipped in between the bed and the mirror. "Come on!" Lynn said, taking her hands to join in the fun.

For the next few minutes they danced and sang to several songs. They were laughing so hard that Lynn forgot for a moment where they were. The bed groaned behind them when they bumped into it.

It was only when a head popped in at the open doorway that they stopped.

Thomas was looking in, shaking his head.

When he left, they kept dancing.

Lynn could never tell her daughter the dreams she'd had when she was Sara's age. Back then she'd felt limitless and light, just like this music. Lynn had always been able to sing. But she never had an *American Idol* to audition for. She never had parents to encourage her.

Lynn smiled. "You're getting good."

"Thanks, Mom."

She held Sara's hands and somewhere deep down she made another promise to herself. *My children are going to have more opportunities than I had. And it doesn't start with a full checking account or a full pantry but with a full heart.*

Chance Encounter

Kevin always wanted to sing songs, the memorable kind that told stories. The stories of dusty roads and dirty saloons. Did the world even have saloons anymore? Songs that spun tales of Texans who liked to spit and Mexicans who liked to barter and Coloradoans who still searched for gold. He would play his guitar and sing in the smoky dim light.

But it was the afternoon after another busy day of work and all Kevin could do was turn up the stereo in his car. All he could do was hum to the latest song on his favorite station that jammed classic and contemporary country music. All he could do was drive on suburban roads in nice cutout neighborhoods with nice cutout lives. Sometimes when he was driving in the country and the windows were shut in his car, or he was in his house when it was just him, he'd crank Alan Jackson and he'd mimic playing the guitar and sing and live just a little. Nobody needed to see him. Nobody needed to know how ridiculous he looked.

In the country, he could look ridiculous and the country wouldn't know. Or care. But out here, it was different. Out here, soccer moms stared at him with humor as he rocked out in his car.

The phone vibrated and Kevin answered it.

"You almost home?"

"Yeah. Almost." He smiled. "I'm going to Target to look for a digital camera. Remember?"

"Oh, yeah," she said.

He often joked that the twins were draining her brain cells, and Jenny half agreed.

"Do you want to pick up some dinner?" Jenny asked.

"Only if it's something really greasy, since I'm eating for three," Kevin said.

"You should be so lucky."

They talked about options for several minutes. Jenny took a long time before not deciding anything. "You decide. You know what I like."

Baby A is named Forgetfulness and Baby B is named Indecision.

"All right," Kevin said, still amused. "See you soon."

*

He wasn't sure how this went, buying a digital camera for the kid named Thomas. How much was he supposed to spend? If they were on a budget, he might be able to nail down the exact amount. But it was a bit like asking a sailor how much he could eat and drink while going down on a sinking ship. The question seemed a bit ridiculous in light of everything.

After looking for twenty minutes, Kevin found a nice Canon that was about eighty bucks, almost half its original price. He could have gotten a less expensive camera or a less-known brand, but something in him wanted to do this.

Am I concerned that Thomas gets a nice camera or that I look good?

That question was even more ridiculous. Thomas would never know who was giving him these gifts. That was kind of the whole point, wasn't it? Giving without getting anything in return.

Kevin had so much to learn and so far to go.

"Uncle Kevin?"

He hadn't heard that term in some time. When he glanced up he saw the smiling face of his niece Kaylee.

"I'm sorry, do I know you?" he joked as he walked over and gave the sixteen-year-old a hug. "What are you doing here?"

"I love shopping here. Getting a new camera?"

"Uh, yeah."

He thought back to the last time he'd seen Kaylee. A year ago Thanksgiving, since they traded off years between sides of the family.

Has it really been a year?

"You never reply to me on Facebook," Kaylee said.

"I'm never on Facebook. Seriously."

Kevin couldn't believe how grown up the young girl had become. Kaylee was his sister's only child. Jill had tried to have another but she had ended up having two miscarriages. He wasn't extremely close to Jill, his younger and only sibling, and that meant that he barely knew this young girl standing in front of him.

She's a young woman.

"How's your mother?" he asked.

"She's doing good."

"And how's school going?"

The blond-haired girl smiled when answering, "Just getting ready for the big play."

"That's right."

Yeah, the one we got an invite for and never responded to. Hope she doesn't—

"I hope you guys can come and see it," Kaylee said.

She was so excited to say this that it almost shamed him.

"Yeah, we'd like to. I really hope we can. Just depends on the babies, you know."

How long are you going to use that excuse?

"Just think," Kaylee told him in an animated way. "How many *Christmas Carols* are you going to see where Scrooge is actually a woman?"

Kevin laughed. "I get it now."

The high school play was called *A Christmas Carole.* He'd been too busy, as usual, to notice that it was a modern take on the classic story.

So that's why Jill was so excited that Kaylee got the lead role.

"So is 'Carole' an old lady?"

"Not as old as Scrooge. We've made it up-to-date. She's still old, kinda like you."

"Ouch," Kevin said. "Yeah, that's ancient."

"There's going to be three shows you can come to."

Come on, Kev, step up to the plate.

"We'll be there. I'll let your mom know which time."

"Oh, that's awesome." The nephews on Jenny's side of the

family were much more subdued and laid-back. "I know you're going to like it. It's really funny. Kinda like some of those videos you guys have made."

"You've seen them?"

"Yeah, sure. Mom's shown them to me."

That was a surprise. But so was this chance encounter with his niece he hadn't seen in almost a year.

"Tell your mom hi and that I'll call, okay?"

"Can't wait to see the twins!"

"Yeah, me, too, except I hope it'll be sometime in the new year before they arrive," Kevin said as he told her good-bye.

So much to do and so little time remaining to do it.

Story of my life.

A New Song

She was a beautiful love song but one he would never be able to sing. He was simply a silly campfire song sung by a bunch of punch-drunk boys who could never remember the lyrics. The two didn't belong together. Not in any way.

Yet still, in some strange way, it really seemed as if Cass liked him. And his surprising newfound friend and occasional mechanic, Carlos, was trying to prove this point over lunch break.

A lunch break where Thomas was sitting with Carlos and his friends. His *football* friends. For the second day in a row.

It had started the day after the Maxima incident. Thomas was trying to find a shell to crawl into like a turtle when he saw the big guy laughing with some of his other big friends. When it seemed like Carlos recognized him, Thomas wanted to start walking the other way.

"Hey—you—whatever your name—come 'ere."

When Thomas got to the table, he was glad to see that someone else recognized him. It was a senior named Juan he remembered playing basketball with.

"You're the basketball player, right?"

Thomas nodded as five guys stared at him. Not in a dismissive way or even a judgmental way but more curious, sorta like they were watching a commercial on television.

Kinda noticing it and kinda not.

"I told you about him, man," Juan said to Carlos. "He's the guy that schooled West on the court, the one who got the bloody nose."

"West hit you?" Carlos asked him.

"Is that Vic's last name?"

"Yeah."

"Then yeah, he landed one."

Carlos said what appeared to be a curse word in Spanish and then nodded for Thomas to sit down. He felt a bit awkward sitting in the middle of all these guys, but then again he always felt awkward. It was nice to have people asking him to sit with them.

Everything changed, of course, when the group of girls walked up to their table and stopped.

It was Julia, a dark-skinned senior who looked like a model, especially on days when she wore short skirts, like today. There was another senior that Thomas thought was named Alexis but he wasn't sure, and then Cass stood in the middle.

The guys called out to Julia and remarked on her outfit. Thomas couldn't help blushing, glad nobody was really paying him any attention.

Then he noticed Cass looking at him longer than a millisecond.

"You're the new guy, right?" she asked him as the others talked back and forth.

He nodded.

And I've been new for a whole year.

"Where are you from again?"

She was confident and friendly.

And beautiful.

"Georgia."

Her eyes were even bluer this close up. They reminded him of that song "Blue and Bluer." They just kept getting bluer the more he looked at her.

"And why'd you move to Greer, then?"

To find my wife and settle down, a silly voice in his head said.

"My mom. Changed work."

And that was it. That was all. The conversation switched, the guys kept teasing—or harassing, depending on how one looked at it—Julia about her little skirt, and then the girls left.

Now, a day later, Carlos was telling Thomas what he'd heard, even though Thomas thought this was a cruel joke.

"She's a junior who looks like a junior in college," Thomas said, more to remind himself than to remind Carlos.

"Doesn't matter. It's obvious she thinks you're cute."

"No it isn't." It couldn't be. There was no possible way.

Carlos talked with his mouth full as he shrugged his massive shoulders. "She said it. She said those words. What else can that mean?"

"She probably says that about everybody."

"Cass ignores most of the boys around here. She's a cheerleader, so that's why she's nice to us. She has to be."

Thomas still didn't believe it. There had to be some logical explanation.

"It's because I'm new," Thomas said. "It's because she thinks there's more to me than meets the eye."

"Okay." It was obvious that Carlos didn't really care if Cass did indeed like Thomas. He'd just mentioned it because he thought it was funny. Some kind of joke. "So, then, go with it. Pretend like there's more to you."

Guys could be oblivious. They could ignore things like what happened to the car the other day, or the fact that Thomas wore the same pair of jeans every day. They could care less that Thomas never mentioned where he lived or what his family did.

But girls weren't oblivious. Girls liked knowing things. They liked *details.* Especially girls like Cass.

It's just because I'm a new face in the hallways. That's it.

"I don't think so," Thomas said.

"Fine, whatever," Carlos said with a shrug. "Don't you think she's hot?"

"It's not that."

"I can talk to her if you want me to."

The fact that Cass might be interested in him—and that was a very big *might be*—was maybe just as surprising as Carlos being so nice to him. The guy was a big jock but he was also kindhearted. It was obvious that he didn't care what people thought.

But girls always care. Always.

"Don't worry about it," Thomas said to Carlos.

Don't worry about it because it's all in your head.

All Thomas could think of was the truth—he didn't want people to know, especially people like Cass. He'd seen her driving a nice car. He'd never seen her in the same outfit. And yes, he paid attention to things like that. Not because this was some silly teen movie about the rich girl and the poor guy but because he liked details, and he liked seeing what kind of outfits fit her mood and her style. He liked her mood and her style. Sometimes late at night, when he was in bed, he'd close his eyes and picture Cass smiling at him.

Cass was always the same in each dream. She was that breathtaking junior he got to see a few times each day. Yet *he* was always different in those dreams. Cass and Greer High and everybody else was the same, but Thomas was someone else living someone else's life.

And in that dream, he could sing a new song. He had the lyrics memorized and he sang it with a beautiful voice.

Serenity

"*You gotta be* kidding me."

Of course, Lynn knew that Murphy wasn't kidding her. He'd never promised her a permanent job when she applied. She'd never promised him that she'd be around long either, since she was constantly looking for a better job.

The only question had been who would end this temporary relationship first.

"You know how little work I got as is."

As if to demonstrate his point, they were talking in the main dining area. It was eight o'clock on a Wednesday night and not a soul was around except the two of them.

"Does it have to be right now?" Lynn asked. "I just spent four hundred bucks to fix my car. Four hundred bucks I needed for other bills."

"Lynn, I'm sorry, really. But this ain't the Salvation Army."

You grubby old . . .

That was when she shut down, when she nodded and held her tongue.

For a moment she thought of the Serenity Prayer. She knew

it well from the first time she'd left Daryl. She hadn't really, truly left him, but she'd threatened him. It had been after a really bad weekend where he blacked out drunk, woke up to beat her, then disappeared with the car. When he showed back up at home, Lynn gave him an ultimatum: drinking or family. The Daryl back then was younger and softer and for a while he sobered up.

He was sober for twenty-seven days. And in those twenty-seven days, when he would attend AA and smoke a lot and drink a lot of coffee, Daryl would be reciting the Serenity Prayer all the time.

She needed to hear that prayer, even if in her head it was in the voice of her husband. Or ex-husband, whatever the case might be.

God, grant me the serenity to accept the things I cannot change, courage to change the things I can, and wisdom to know the difference.

She wondered if crusty old Murphy knew the Serenity Prayer. Did he even know what serenity was? He looked hard and older than someone in his fifties. "If I could do anything, I would," he said to her.

That's what they all say.

The prayer lingered in her head, but it sounded more like a slogan or a commercial than anything else. It wasn't personal, and it certainly wasn't a prayer she was actually praying to God.

Maybe a real prayer would help. But she had a ways to go before she could come to God with all her baggage.

*

"I thought you were supposed to work today," Sara said.

Children had a way of making moments like this even more difficult.

Lynn had wanted to wait until after dinner, but that looked impossible now. Sara waited for an answer.

Thomas was just walking in from school. He glanced at her, then stood watching.

Does my face give it away that clearly?

"I lost my job."

"For real?" Thomas asked.

"For good?" Sara asked.

"Yes. And yes."

"Does that mean we have stay *here* a lot longer?"

"Sara, I've told you that we're not going to be able to move for some time."

"So what are we going to do for dinner?"

Sara had a one-track mind, and that was food. Wasn't it supposed to be boys who thought like that? But a dark shade fell over Thomas's face. He knew what her news meant. He walked into the living room with his eyes down.

I was the one who brought us here and I have to be the one to figure out how we're going to survive.

"We'll figure something out about dinner," she told Sara as she walked past her to Thomas. "It'll be okay."

"Says who?" Thomas asked.

She was surprised by his sudden and frustrated response.

"I do."

"Okay."

But that was his teenage I'll-believe-it-when-I-see-it voice talking.

She loved her kids but they were still just that—kids. They couldn't act any older than they were. Thomas was still a teen, all stifled and unsure and searching for the right words. That indifference didn't mean he was indifferent. He just wasn't sure what else to be or do right now.

I don't know what to do and I'm the grown-up.

Thomas sat down and took off his shoes. Lynn noticed how bad they looked. She knew that one of the gifts he'd asked for was something he badly needed—and desperately wanted.

If she was to start praying, it would be to ask the Lord to get Thomas some decent basketball shoes. He certainly deserved them.

Lynn glanced at her son, so tall and so timid and keeping everything he had inside. Then she glanced at her daughter, every thought expressed on her face, every emotion always a second away from unraveling.

These are my babies, the ones I nursed and promised to forever love and protect and take care of.

She wanted to tell them she was sorry. Not for losing the job, but for leaving their home. She hadn't thought everything through. She had simply been tired and scared and she was tired of being scared.

"I'll find something else soon," she offered instead of an apology.

Thomas didn't look at her, and she let him be for the moment. Sara was looking in the refrigerator, thinking only about her stomach.

Even though both of her kids were only feet away from her, Lynn felt completely alone.

In the corner of the room where an end table used to sit, the bare Christmas tree stood waiting to be adorned with lights and ornaments. It had so much potential to be beautiful, to really be something.

Lynn closed her eyes, not wanting to see the tree anymore.

She knew that she needed more than serenity at this time.

I need a little hope.

Under the Speckled Stars

Thomas slid open the door and slipped out into the night, hoping not to wake Mom and Sara.

After a few moments he exhaled. Thomas hadn't even realized that he was holding his breath as he stepped out of the trailer until now.

He'd finished his homework and was finished reading the latest Dennis Shore novel from the library. As he walked down the dirt driveway, he thought it was nice to be in an area where he could enjoy the still black of night and the dense wilderness of the woods, even if he did feel out of touch living here in this abandoned place.

Even if Dad knew the address, he might not be able to find us.

Sometimes he felt like the trailer represented them, the remnants of the family that used to be. A structure that was just barely hanging on in a place nobody paid any attention to. As he walked the dirt road this late night and saw the dark shapes of cows in the pasture, he wondered if Mom had chosen this place just for its remoteness. They had no phone, no Internet connection. Their television didn't even work because of something to do with a digital something-or-other. Mr. Sinclair had told them he would get them a converter box but so far he hadn't come by with one.

Still, it was nice to be able to walk in privacy and peace and look up at the stars without worrying. Nobody was paying any attention to him. Not here. He felt free under this sky, the cool breeze only adding to the crisp picture above.

As he walked, he heard the flap from his shoe, the same one that kept tearing apart. Superglue didn't really work on soles. Then again, most people would be surprised what could work if you really tried things out.

The jean jacket he wore didn't really keep him warm, even though it sure was tight. He knew this was the last winter it would fit, unless he starved himself. It was tight across the shoulder and arms, and it wasn't because he was pumping iron at the gym.

Thomas wondered what it would be like not to have to think about such things. The flapping tongue of his basketball shoes, the hugging grip of his favorite denim coat. He saw kids every day who played with expensive things without thought. They didn't think about the shoes or the clothes they wore. They didn't wonder about whether they'd eat supper or about the job after school or the rent for this month. They wondered what new apps they could download on their new iPod or iPhone. They checked which movie they'd see even though they'd probably be bored with it as they ate popcorn and drinks that cost as much as he could make working that same amount of time.

Now he had something new to worry about: figuring out a way to support Mom and Sara.

If only he could figure something out. But it was eleven o'clock now. It always seemed like *now* was not on his side. *Later* might be a best buddy, but *now* was an enemy.

He thought stuff like this a lot, but he didn't get angry when he did. His father angered him, or some of the guys at school, or even the fact that the three of them had to move out here in the first place. But he hated pity, especially self-pity. He was healthy and he was relatively smart and he knew that with time and luck he might be able to get out of this place. Not just this exact address—well, yeah, that too—but this place in life.

For a while he thought about Mom's news. This only made him more determined to find a job and contribute. It was good too, because it made the stuff at school seem stupid and silly. Which it really was anyway. He wanted to help out his mom. He wanted to help Sara cheer up. She didn't know how to cope with what was going on, so she went from being mopey to being irritating.

I need to help them out.

He thought about checking back in at the grocery store, using some determination. Maybe that would show the manager he had what it took. He would ask the Parkers about whether he could do any extra work at their house. He might even ask the Sinclairs if there was extra work around the farm.

That'll just be the start. I can make money. There are ways to do it without robbing banks or inventing Facebook.

A cool breeze made him quicken his pace. For a while he wanted to stay outside of the trailer that always smelled like kerosene. Thomas liked being outside, cold but alive and free under the speckled stars.

That was when he prayed the most, on walks like this. Maybe it was just in his imagination, but he felt like God might be able to hear and see him just a little better if he was outside and talking out loud in the silent night under the heavens.

"Dear Lord, please help us," he said. "Help Mom. Give her strength. Help her out. Help us all out. Help Dad too, Lord, whatever he's doing now. And I just pray that you get us through this time. Help Mom to get a job. And help me to figure out how to help her out in whatever way I can."

Help

It was the second Sunday after Thanksgiving and Jenny decided to sleep in after a night of restlessness. She had suggested in a half-comatose state that Kevin take Gregory to church. Gregory loved hanging out with other boys and girls his age in the children's center. And they would have gone to church if it had been up to Gregory. But fortunately, Kevin was the one with the license and the keys to the car. Not to mention the few issues he had with church.

Instead of going to the ten-thirty morning service, Kevin decided to help Jenny out and finish decorating the Christmas tree. This was one of those things that didn't really interest Kevin, that Jenny always did herself. Jenny had decided early on that she could handle the Christmas decorations. He'd tried the first few years of their marriage, but he got fired after doing a subpar job on the tree. Yet everything took longer these days. So the tree was only 50 percent finished.

"What do you say about helping me decorate the tree?" Kevin asked Gregory, who was so overjoyed he gave him a big hug and ran into the living room to start going through the boxes.

It was fantastic. Opening the big boxes only to find smaller boxes containing even smaller boxes with ornaments. Some of the ornaments he didn't recognize, but Gregory loved them, so they used them anyway. Gregory accidentally sat on one, and then he accidentally dropped one on the tile floor. No big deal.

They had found a long string of colored, blinking lights that Gregory wanted to use, so Kevin ended up weaving it alongside the other set of regular lights that Jenny had previously put up.

He wanted to have this all finished for Mommy when she came down the stairs.

When Jenny did finally enter the living room, she looked at the two of them as if they were playing in mud.

"Kev—what are you doing?"

"Mommy—we finished the tree!"

"I see." Jenny couldn't stop looking at the tree.

"We changed things up a little."

"Where'd you get those blinking lights?"

"From the bag," Kevin said.

"And where'd you find those ornaments?"

"Don't you like them?"

She gave him a horrified look but then smiled when Gregory was looking at her. The ornaments were little dogs in Christmas sweaters. Sure, they clashed a bit with her classy burgundy and gold, but maybe this year they could have that hodgepodge of a tree Kevin always told them they should do.

Gregory was opening another box and pulling out some silver garland.

"Sweetie, no, no, don't take that out." Jenny shot Kevin an irritated look.

"I was just—we were just trying to help out," Kevin said.

"Why didn't you guys go to church?"

"I don't know," he said, but Jenny knew exactly.

Because I don't want to sit there and think of my to-do list and hear a pastor tell me all the other things I still need to do.

The lights blinked around the Christmas dogs.

"They're Santa Buddies!" Gregory said.

"Great—I never even saw these."

"I think I bought them last year," Kevin said.

"I see."

Maybe we should've gone to church.

Just as Kevin was about to say something, half a strand of blinking lights flickered quickly, then went out. Jenny shook her head and started to laugh.

*

Later on that morning, after a pancake breakfast that served as a brunch for all of them, Kevin helped Jenny redecorate the tree. Or more like undo the damage he'd done. After finishing most everything on it, Jenny took a break, sitting on a chair in the living room.

"You feeling okay?" he asked.

Such a redundant question.

"I'm sore," Jenny replied.

Such a redundant reply.

"You worried about this week?"

She looked away for a moment, nodding as she did. He knew that she was nervous about the next doctor's appointment. Whenever it crossed his mind, and it seemed to cross his mind all the time, Kevin would begin to worry. Their next appointment was this Wednesday, when Jenny would be thirty-one weeks pregnant.

"I'm just trying not to think about it too much and worry," Jenny said.

Guess it's a good thing I brought it up, huh?

"It'll be fine. I'm sure Baby B has caught up to Baby A."

From her expression he could tell that Jenny not only doubted his comment, but it was obvious she knew that he was just saying it to make her feel better. "We still need to figure out names."

"I keep telling you—Cujo and Maximus. Very masculine names."

"Ha ha."

For some reason, it was easier referring to them as Baby A and Baby B. If something did happen to one or both of them . . .

Stop it, Kev, don't go there.

But deep down underneath the joking, he did worry about something happening to one or both of the babies. They were only at week thirty-one, and the doctor himself had said they were entering a critical stretch in terms of the growth of each baby.

Doesn't matter if they're called Baby A and Baby B or whatever, I love them just like I love Gregory.

Each day this love grew, and with it came fear. A crazy, terrifying kind of fear that was far different from the anxiety of paying bills or finding new work.

Jenny put her hand on her belly. "Whatever we call Baby B, he sure is an active one. Feel."

Kevin put his hand and felt the movement, like slight little kicks.

That's good. You keep at it. You keep stretching and turning and growing. And maybe, God willing, we'll see you and your brother in a short while. Not too short but short enough.

"It's crazy, isn't it?" Kevin said.

Jenny didn't need to ask what "it" referred to. He was touching it. She was it. They were living in it. Every day it showed up at the doorstop. This was their life and it was changing quickly and dramatically.

"I hope he's okay," Jenny finally said.

Kevin didn't need to ask how much it weighed on her. He knew she thought of the babies every other second, especially this little one that wasn't growing the way it should.

I think of them every other second that I'm not thinking of saving the company and trying to keep the employees working for me.

He wanted to tell her to continue to be strong, to keep having faith, that God was going to take care of them. But he couldn't. He couldn't tell her what he himself didn't believe.

Maybe I really should go to church. Maybe then I could have the courage to come before my Maker and ask for a little help.

He hadn't asked for help in a long time. But Kevin knew that eventually, he was going to need as much help as they could get.

Windows

The bell rang and the students filed out of the library, but Thomas sat there, at the desk in the corner, staring at the screen. Staring at himself.

He wasn't sure he could stand up. If he could, he sure didn't want to go back out *there,* out into the wild. Now he could understand why others stayed away from him out there in the hallways and classrooms.

For the entire fourth period before lunch, all fifty minutes, Thomas had sat looking at this Facebook page on Carlos's laptop wondering why. Wondering why and how someone could be so mean and cruel. It didn't make him angry. It just made him sad.

Had this all come from the basketball game and Vic's fear of competition?

I love basketball but there's still more important things in this world than ball.

Maybe someone dropped Vic West on his head when he was young. That had to be why the guy was so mean. So mean and so stupid.

Of course, Thomas wasn't going to tell that to Vic's face.

He was a good-looking guy and seemed to be popular enough.

So why does he hate me so much?

Thomas had known about Vic before the whole thing on the court playing five-on-five. But ever since, he'd started to ask about Vic. Carlos and his football buddies knew him, but certainly didn't seem to care much for him. And that was before this whole thing happened. The more Thomas had gotten to know about Vic, the more it seemed the guy should be welcoming him to Greer High. They seemed to have a lot in common. Vic's parents were divorced, so he lived with his father. Thomas would guess he didn't have much of a house. Vic drove his father's pickup when he could, but the rusted-out Chevy revealed they didn't have a lot of money. Maybe they had a little more than Thomas and his family, but not much.

Thomas thought a guy like that would give him some slack.

So he thought until Carlos pulled him aside before second period earlier this morning.

"Man you ain't gonna believe this," Carlos had said.

The guy wore loose jeans under his football jersey. He reached into a pocket and found an iPhone. Thomas might be able to get one of those in about ten years.

Yeah, maybe that exact model too, ten years from now.

Carlos's thick hands were surprisingly nimble in using his phone. He touched the screen, then gave Thomas the phone.

"I'm assuming you haven't seen this."

Thomas recognized that he was looking at Facebook. He used to get on it back in Georgia, but it had been months since he'd checked out his page.

The page Carlos was showing him had his picture on it. But this wasn't his own personal profile.

"What is this?" he asked.

He kept scrolling and reading. To the right of the picture, obviously taken in the hallways at school, was some text:

Feed the Hungry

Tom Brandt is a new kid at Greer High School. As these pictures show, he is in dire need of food, clothing, and A LIFE. If we get 1,000 followers we'll buy Tom a whole new wardrobe. And maybe lunch.

For a second Thomas couldn't understand what he was looking at. He thought Carlos was playing around with him. "What is this?"

"It's a joke, that's what it is." Carlos took the phone from him and touched it for a few moments. "There—look at that."

There were a dozen shots of Tom on different days. He was wearing the same jeans in all the pictures, with a few different shirts.

"What—? I don't . . ."

Carlos nodded as if he knew exactly what Thomas was going to say. Or what he was going to try to say.

"Who took these?" Thomas asked, suddenly feeling frantic.

Carlos showed him the screen again.

Sure enough, the "creator" of this page was none other than Vic West.

Thomas felt bewildered for a moment, trying to figure out what this meant. He didn't believe it even though he could see it with his own eyes.

"If he wasn't part of the basketball team, I swear we'd kick his butt," Carlos said.

There were over a hundred people who "liked" the page.

A hundred students actually pressed a button to say they liked this page?

"We can get the guy to get rid of it. Or a teacher will if I don't. I can't stand that Vic. He's a rat."

Thomas's bewilderment suddenly turned into something else.

Shame.

He felt naked standing here.

Sure enough, the jeans that he wore in every one of those photos were the ones he was wearing now. Same for the shirt he had on.

"Thanks for showing me," he said, wanting to slip away to a locker and lock himself in it.

"I can say something to someone . . ."

At least he had Carlos and his buddies looking out for him.

"No, it's okay," Thomas said. "Really."

"All I gotta do is just *talk* to Vic. I don't care that he plays basketball. I hate that sport anyway."

This was starting to get bigger than just a simple pickup game and a stupid rivalry.

"No, really, it's okay," Thomas said.

Carlos said nothing.

"Thanks for showing me."

"No problem," Carlos said. "Just—just let me know if you need anything."

"Thanks."

Before Carlos had left, Thomas asked him if he could borrow his laptop for a couple of periods before lunch. Carlos obliged, probably because he felt so sorry for him. Thomas wanted to check out the page more carefully but didn't want to do it on a public computer where other kids could see.

When Carlos said good-bye, Thomas was left in the sea of students who walked by him.

They all knew.

Need anything? Carlos's words rang.

Thomas felt as if he were walking in a muddy swamp, his clothes and face dirty, and everybody else was watching from the shore. Watching and laughing.

*

It took two whole periods before he found his footing.

In the library, Thomas had logged onto Facebook and seen the various comments on the page that Vic West had created specifically to mock Thomas.

For the entire period he had felt paralyzed and stunned. But he was starting to think again, starting to breathe again, starting to figure it out again.

There might be a lot of things in this world that Thomas lacked. But self-respect wasn't one of them. He had that.

Everybody in this school can "like" this stupid Facebook page. Doesn't change who I am. Doesn't change one thing.

For the rest of the day, Thomas couldn't help thinking and wondering what to do about the Facebook situation.

One reason he'd never gotten into Facebook was because he didn't have a computer or Internet service.

But the other reason was this: he didn't want to see other kids' lives and he didn't want to share his.

If he had a digital camera to take a picture with, what would he photograph? The fire-scarred field behind their trailer? The closetlike room he slept in? The chipped and corroded floors? The sad expression on Sara's face?

Obviously I don't need any more pics of myself, since there are already plenty out there.

He didn't want to see the kids with their big families going on big vacations to pretty places. *Look, Mom, I'm on the Jet Ski! Look, Dad, I'm tan!* He knew what golf courses and country clubs looked like, even if it was just in his imagination. He could picture beaches all the way to heaven itself. He didn't need to see them on pages and pages belonging to kids, most of whom were now distant memories at his former high school.

That would only make him sad.

Thomas didn't want to live life sad or in want.

Looking into store windows at things he didn't and couldn't have only made things worse.

So he chose to avoid those windows altogether.

It is what it is.

That's what his aunt said all the time, the same aunt who'd lost a husband and a daughter, the same aunt who moved to New York to try to leave everything else behind.

It is what it is, and I can't do a thing about it.

That was the window Thomas wanted to look into. That was the picture Thomas wanted to be a part of. That was the life he wanted—a life with no regret, a life of hope and faith. And yes, joy.

Lots of people probably didn't appreciate this thing called *joy*. But Thomas did. He treasured that word.

Joy wasn't something someone could buy or make.

Joy was something that only God could create.

Sitting in the uncomfortable seat on the loud bus home, Thomas realized that the only way to combat ignorance and hatred would be to show joy.

And that gave way to another idea. A crazy idea that made him smile.

Stuck in Traffic

Kevin dropped Jenny off in front of the hospital for her ultrasound and parked the car.

For a moment he stayed in his seat, hesitant to get out.

He didn't want to know. He was afraid to know the truth.

It was one thing to go into a room and discover the fate of your job and livelihood. It was a whole other thing to meet with a doctor and find out the fate of the two growing lives in their mother's belly.

He shut his eyes for a moment.

"God, please be with her. Be with those babies. Give us some good news. Let them be okay. Especially Baby B."

As Kevin climbed out of the car and felt a cold blast of wind moving across the parking lot, he thought of what he'd be doing if Gregory were with him. Kevin would be holding his hand, making sure his son didn't run ahead and in front of some oncoming car. Gregory would be at his side, and Daddy would be guiding him patiently toward the sidewalk.

Just like God the Father.

It was that simple.

Why shouldn't it be?

I'm holding your hand and I'm walking right beside you, Kevin. Don't you see that?

The problem wasn't God's lack of care, it was Kevin's desire to control and his pride.

I'm a grown man who doesn't need his hand held and shouldn't be this paranoid and scared about life and these twins.

Kevin tried to let go and see the truth he'd always been taught in the church: that God was watching over Jenny. God could see every tiny little cell of those boys inside of her. He knew their names and how fast their hearts pulsed and how long they would live and what they would do with their lives.

But I don't know and I'm scared, God—I'm honestly terrified.

Then he imagined God's hand, so firm and so strong. A hand that wouldn't let him step out in front of a moving car, a hand that wasn't going to let him bolt ahead, a hand that held him safe and secure.

But I've made it clear for some time that I didn't want my hand held. What then? Does God finally let go?

Sometimes he saw others whose faith resembled a warm blanket, covering them in security from the cold winter's night. Jenny's faith was like that—steady, silent, and secure. Kevin's faith was more like a bedsheet that had been mauled by a stray, hungry dog. It was barely there anymore, hanging together by tiny threads.

Kevin kept thinking of it as he entered the hospital and went to find Jenny. "Please, God," he prayed again, "give us some good news."

Statements like this were uttered all the time as easily as

"Good morning" and "See you later." They were tossed out like pennies into a fountain.

Kevin hoped that these prayers were a little more valuable. That they would be heard and somehow answered.

*

An hour later, as Kevin and Jenny sat in the doctor's office, he thought that maybe his prayers had gotten stuck in the busy traffic of holiday prayers. He sat holding Jenny's hand, seeing the tears on her cheeks and the desperate look in her eyes. He sat trying to be strong but knowing that it was just an act for her, knowing he needed to try to convince Jenny that he wasn't absolutely terrified.

It was the news that they'd feared the most.

Baby B wasn't growing.

They had hoped that perhaps Baby B was a late bloomer, but the measurements told a more alarming story. The weight discrepancy between A and B had increased. Even the always-positive Dr. Kalchbrenner seemed more reserved and more careful about the words he spoke.

"We've talked about this before, but since you elected not to have an amniocentesis done, there are certain things we can't rule out. We can still do one if you want us to."

"No," Jenny quickly said. "We already decided—we've gone this long without getting one."

"I understand," the doctor said in his patient tone. "But it would give you peace of mind."

They had already decided not to get an amniocentesis due to the very minute possibility that it could hurt the babies. Why chance it if it wasn't going to change anything anyway? They were having these children and nothing through the process was going to make them think otherwise.

"Of course there is a chance—a very good chance—that the two babies are normal and healthy and this little guy is just smaller," Dr. Kalchbrenner said. "I spent my whole life being in the lower percentile—I'm shorter than most guys, so I get it. It's just that when there is a discrepancy like this between twins, we grow increasingly worried that it could be something else. It can be nothing, or it could be a problem with the placenta and how much oxygen Baby B is getting. Or it could be a chromosome abnormality."

Jenny shook her head and tightened her lips as she continued to cry. She looked at Kevin, who squeezed her hand and mouthed the words, "It's going to be okay."

"What does that mean?" Jenny said with a wavering voice. "Does that mean I might have them soon?"

"We're going to want to see you weekly to see exactly how each baby is doing."

Wait a minute.

"So it could be any day?" Kevin asked.

The doctor nodded and continued talking in a calm but serious tone about wanting to make sure they did everything possible for both the babies. He talked about rare cases when one baby begins to decline, jeopardizing the life of the other.

But that means there is a possibility for the unthinkable . . .

They agreed to meet next week to monitor Jenny and the babies. Kevin and Jenny could come in earlier if anything else changed. The doctor left them in his office for a moment, giving them some privacy. Kevin embraced Jenny as she wept in his arms.

"They're going to be okay," he told her.

"What if something happens to them?"

"Don't worry." He rubbed her back, trying to stay as positive as possible. "You're going to be okay."

"I'm scared."

He just held her and understood.

There was nothing more he wanted than to hold these babies and make sure that they were okay. He wasn't sure that Jenny could take losing them.

And God knows I'm not strong enough to be there for her if something like that happens.

Kevin wanted to believe that his hand was being held by someone in control. He really did.

Yet that desperate falling sensation he felt in his soul made him believe something else.

Flawed and Broken

The man in the baggy, worn overalls standing across the room from Lynn had been reasonable and generous to let them move into the trailer a year ago. But Lynn knew that his generosity had limits. Mr. Sinclair was tough. She could see it in his eyes. He knew a thing or two about people. She didn't need to argue with what he'd said. She already expected it even before showing up at his door early this morning to talk about the rent.

"I appreciate everything you've done," Lynn said.

The wrinkled face watching her didn't react. "Done nothing at all. Just didn't quite know all the work the place needed. Mighta reconsidered if I'd a known."

"We're glad you didn't."

"I can give you until the first of the year, but then I need to get paid."

Lynn nodded. "I understand."

"Always wanted to do something about that trailer but never got around to it. Wasn't worth the money to fix it up. But not sure it's worth the rent."

"Your money will be coming," Lynn said.

She hadn't told Mr. Sinclair everything. In fact, all she had told him was that the rent was going to be later than usual, that she would probably not be able to pay until the end of the month. Lynn had neglected to tell him about losing her job.

Because hopefully I'll find something new by then.

"I know that your boy asked about some work. I'll let 'im know as soon as I have anything."

She couldn't believe it. Not that Thomas had asked Mr. Sinclair for more work, but that he had done it so quickly.

"Thank you," she said.

"It's tough supporting a family, ain't it?"

She nodded. He had never once asked her what her story was. He had never asked her if she had family around or where her husband was or anything. He had simply understood that she needed help.

Before Lynn left, Mr. Sinclair called out her name.

"Hold on a sec," he said.

He disappeared and then came back with a wrapped box.

"It's a Christmas present."

"No—please—we should be the ones giving you guys something."

"Oh, it's nothing. Liz wanted y'all to have some jelly. Hope you like jelly, 'cause there's a lot of it in there. She makes it from scratch. Think it's twelve jars or somethin' like that."

"Thank you. Yes, we love jelly."

"Well, yeah, me too, but doesn't make the fanciest Christmas present."

"Your patience has been enough of a present," Lynn said. "Thank you."

*

There was a reason Lynn had not brought the kids to see her family in Greer. Both of her parents were deceased, and her younger sister had moved to New York. Jesse, her older brother, was the only person left. And that was the primary problem.

"Why do you never want to go see them?" Thomas had asked.

The question had been honest, but it had brought up a lot of bad memories. She had always said that she'd lost touch with her brother but Thomas wasn't buying this.

"What if something happens?" he had asked her.

"If what happens?"

"Like you don't find a job—like we can't live here anymore? What if we have to go live with them?"

"No."

She would rather go back home to Georgia than to suddenly show up at her brother's front door. After trying to explain the reasons why to Thomas, she figured that she would simply show him. A part of her wanted him to understand this part of her life, this part of their family.

Another part of her thought that maybe Thomas was right. What if she didn't have enough money to pay for December's rent? What if January came and they were in the same boat? Where would they go?

You have to do what you have to do.

So they made plans to go over to Uncle Jesse's house for dinner.

It took about ten minutes until she realized there was no way on God's green earth that they were going to move there.

Uncle Jesse had two pit bulls that were so crazed they seemed rabid. Their yelping lasted the entire time Lynn and the children were there. Jesse didn't say much about the dogs, but he would occasionally yell out a curse at them. They were on leashes on opposite sides of a backyard that was littered with garbage and car parts. Lynn wasn't sure if the dogs were barking at each other or in unison at her. They had cuts and scratches all over their bodies, making her think maybe her brother took them fighting.

Nothing would surprise her about Jesse. Nothing.

But soon she was surprised.

"Wanna see my Gatling gun?" he asked Thomas.

It was before dinner and they were all in the kitchen that smelled of fried chicken and fried okra. Jesse's two kids were younger than Thomas and Sara. They had only made one appearance before heading back into the family room to watch television. Thomas and Sara stayed in the kitchen, where their uncle Jesse and aunt Susan talked as if they came over all the time, shifting conversation from one random subject to the next.

When Jesse mentioned the gun, Thomas acted like he wasn't sure what his uncle had said.

"Come on. I'll show all of you."

In the backyard, behind the debris of tires and engine parts and car doors and other various pieces belonging to long-lost cars, a leaning woodshed somehow stood. Next to it, under a tarp held down by chunks of firewood and string, an old Volkswagen sat on four cinder blocks.

"First I'll show you a nice little project I made," Jesse said.

He led them into the woodshed that appeared more cluttered than the backyard. If Lynn hadn't grown up with the rotund, balding man with the jeans that kept slipping down, she might have been terrified of going into a woodshed with him. But Jesse was harmless. Well, mostly harmless.

"I rigged this here up the other day. Take a look."

Near the top of the doorway was a rattrap next to a good-sized hole in the wall. A string was attached to the trap's wire and ran along the wood and outside through another opening.

"This 'ere's gonna surprise someone someday."

"What is that?" Sara asked as she looked up at the strange creation above them.

"That's my trap. Someone stole the tires off my Volkswagen not long ago, and I figure they're gonna come back for the windshield."

"What's the mousetrap do?" Lynn asked, afraid to hear the answer but strangely fascinated at the same time.

Jesse scratched his belly underneath his T-shirt. Lynn wondered if this was really happening, if this man was really related to her, if he was just trying to be ultraredneck on purpose.

"I nailed that there rattrap up there after drillin' a hole through the rafter. The hole's about the size of a shotgun shell and it's aimed at the VW. Got a twelve-gauge shotgun shell in there right now, just waiting. But the shell's full a' rock salt and tattoo ink. Tied that there string to the arm of the rattrap—the string goes all the way to my bedroom window. That thief comes back I'm gonna tattoo his behind so I know who he is."

"Jess," Lynn said in complete disbelief.

"What?" He looked totally baffled by her concern.

"So that thing could go off? Now?"

"Sure. If I make it go off."

"What if someone accidentally set it off?" she asked. "Like one of the kids."

"Nah. Look at you. Nervous as always." Jesse giggled in a high-pitched tone that still made him sound like a teenager.

He hasn't matured at all since he turned thirteen.

"Why not just call the police on the guy?" she asked.

"It's a matter of principle."

Lynn nodded.

"If that don't work, well, then I'll just get out the big gun."

Sure enough, there in the corner of the woodshed was a Gatling gun that sat on wheels like a thin cannon. The barrels were long, the handle of it looked like something out of a *Terminator* movie. If, of course, one overlooked the duct tape.

"This'll do the trick," Jesse said, proceeding to use colorful language to describe how he'd colorfully spray the colorful intruder all over his colorful lawn.

"Tell me that's not loaded."

Jesse shook his head, then showed them a tin pail full of massive bullets the length of her hand that were supposed to go into the gun.

That cemented her decision to never, *ever* stay with Jesse and his family.

Lynn just wondered if she needed to call someone. Like the authorities. Or the psych ward.

Later on, as they sat down for dinner, Lynn noticed the carved-out coconut in the middle of the table.

First a rattrap armed with buckshot, then a Gatling gun, now a coconut centerpiece?

"Let's all give thanks to Fred," Jesse said, then winked at Lynn as he closed his eyes and started to pray. "Chicken's yummy in our tummies. Amen."

Lynn glanced at Sara, who was looking at her uncle as if he was from another planet. Thomas had another look on his face—one of complete bewilderment.

"And who's Fred?" Lynn asked.

"I'm Fred, you fruitcake," Jesse said without moving his lips and pointing at the coconut as if he was the world's worst ventriloquist. "He's the head of the table. Here, you gotta come around here to see his face."

Sure enough, Fred the talking coconut, the so-called head of the table, had a painted-on face.

Lynn glanced at Thomas and wondered if he'd seen enough. If he finally understood why she'd never once thought of moving in with this man.

Crazy had a name and it started with *J*.

*

For a while all the three of them could do during the car ride back home was laugh. They were laughing so hard that Lynn had to slow down on the back road because her eyes were tearing up so bad.

"Now you know," Lynn said when she finally composed herself.

"Know what?" Sara asked.

"Why we didn't move in with your uncle Jesse."

"What do you mean?" Thomas asked in full-fledged sarcasm. "It'd be awesome living there."

"Yeah, if you wanted to get shot."

She couldn't help that last remark. It made them all laugh again.

"Why would someone come steal the glass in that car?" Sara asked.

"People will steal anything," Lynn said. "It's just—I doubt they'd ever come on his property looking for something to steal."

"I saw a pair of tires," Thomas said. "They looked new. Maybe we should sneak over there and steal them. We could use them."

"It's a mayater of preencepal," Lynn said, trying to capture her brother's accent.

"Why don't you talk that way?" Thomas asked.

"Because I try. Or maybe because your father rescued me from living here."

"How did Dad rescue you?" Sara asked from the backseat.

Lynn let out a sigh and knew that the laughter had been great medicine for recent days.

"Your father's family—now, they were poor. Didn't have anything. I never saw his pop smile. Never saw him sober either. When we started dating, your father promised me we were going to get away and see the real world."

"So where'd you guys go?"

"Georgia." Lynn couldn't help smiling. "Atlanta was the real world, at least to your father. Anywhere outside of Greer, South Carolina, was the real world. He didn't want to end up like his father. Or like my family."

"So what happened?" Thomas asked her.

"Thomas . . ." It wasn't the question itself that Lynn didn't like, but the way Thomas had said it.

He just stared at her in the passenger seat, waiting for a response.

"Your father was different. He was different than all of them."

For a moment she stared at the headlights cutting through the dark wilderness. No streetlights illuminated their drive back home. This was the country. The dark, lonely country, the kind she had once escaped.

But the darkness found us. It followed us and found us.

"Your father was a lot like you when I first met him," Lynn said.

"How?"

"Just—in a lot of ways, actually."

"Then . . ."

"What happened?" she finished for him. "I don't know. Sometimes we can't escape our roots. Sometimes you can get away but you still can't change who you are at the core."

"That mean I'm going to end up like Dad? Or Uncle Jesse?"

"No," she said quickly. "It means that moving doesn't always solve your problems."

Even in the darkness of the car, she could see her son glance at her with a look that said, *No duh, Mom.*

"So he wasn't always like that?" Thomas asked.

She glanced in the back and saw that Sara was still listening to them in the shadows.

"Like what?"

"Mean."

"No. Thomas—no. Your father wasn't always like that. Now, *his* father, yes. That man was the meanest son of a gun on the face of this earth. That's what your father wanted to get away from. His family. My family. All of the craziness."

"Then what happened?"

The car stopped at a stop sign. Lynn paused for a moment before answering.

"Sometimes life is harder than you expect it will be when you get older."

"I don't ever want to get older," Sara said suddenly.

"Yeah, kinda stinks, huh?" Lynn said.

"No," Thomas said, looking at her. "Dad's the one that stinks."

She tapped his leg with her hand. "Your father isn't a bad man. He just—times are hard. And he's like the rest of us. He's flawed and broken. Sometimes it's hard to let others pick up the pieces."

"Mom—how can you say that after everything?" Thomas asked.

"Are we going to go back home?" Sara added.

"No—I just . . . No, Sara, we're not going back home. No. We're—we're going to figure something out. We might have to move."

"With Uncle Jesse?"

"No," she answered Thomas. "No—not there either."

"So, then what are our options?"

"I don't know. I just—well, I'd prefer not living with someone who has pit bulls and a Gatling gun."

They reached their trailer, a black box that looked more like a lone railroad car off its tracks. Lynn turned toward both Thomas and Sara before shutting off the car.

"I want you both to listen to me and listen good. Don't hate your father. We're all sinful and God is working in all of us. You, me, Sara, your father."

"Is Daddy going to get better?" Sara asked.

"It's harder to change when you get older," Lynn said. "I don't know why that is. Sometimes you just have to hit bottom before you realize some things. And then—some people never change."

"Do you think he will?" Thomas asked.

"I don't know. I really don't know."

Doug's Bike Shop

He was a motivational poster gone bad.

Kevin remembered the generic posters adorning the walls of the company he worked at years ago. Not only were they simplistic designs that he and his colleagues could have arranged in their sleep, but the posters bore clichés like "Some people dream of success . . . while others wake up and work hard at it." It would have some moving, pithy photo attached to it, like a green on a golf course with early-morning dew glistening on it or a crew of a ship guiding their vessel during a raging storm.

He thought of this now in his office as he surveyed a humorous, antimotivational Web site for a laugh. This was one of his outlets. A cheap laugh, but sometimes that was all it took.

There was the Ambition poster that said, "The journey of a thousand miles sometimes ends very, very badly." It showed a fish swimming upstream as a bear waited.

That's not just hilarious, it's true.

"Not everyone gets to be an astronaut when they grow up"—attached to an image of a man making McDonald's french fries.

Or his favorite. "Because nothing says 'You're a loser' more than owning a motivational poster about being a winner"—attached to a poster that said "Winners" with a photo of hands raising a trophy.

Sometimes you worked as hard as you could and nothing came of it. It would be great if life always worked out in neat and tidy ways, but the older Kevin grew, the more he understood the whole notion of "life isn't fair." It wasn't just something that was nice to tell children when they weren't able to buy that fancy bike in the store. Life was indeed very not fair.

Yet what do I have to complain about, anyway?

If he never went outside of this office, then yes, he could complain. He could talk about the lack of clients recently and the lack of bills paid by those clients who had stayed. He could talk about the very real possibility of losing his staff or, worse yet, losing the company he'd worked so hard to build.

But if he was to get off the nice leather chair he owned and open the door and start walking outside, he'd get a different perspective. He didn't have to walk very far to find someone more hurting, more broken, and more full of despair.

His buddy Seth, for instance, who was going through a bitter divorce from his wife of fourteen years along with needing to find a new job after just being laid off.

Or there was Kevin's other friend Ray, who was going through the same situation *with* kids.

The day could be darker, he had to admit. If Kevin was stuck in these four walls looking at a monitor and hearing the silence echoing off the voices in his head, it was easy to start worrying and wondering. But once he got up and started looking at life around him, he saw more.

He not only saw despair, but he also saw hope.

Hope in the smallest of places.

Hope in people like Oscar. Good old Oscar, who probably didn't even know what a motivational poster looked like.

Oscar was an elderly African-American man about six feet two inches who had a voice like a raspy blues singer. He wore a wool trench coat year-round. He kept gum in his pockets that he'd give to the kids in the neighborhood. Each piece of gum would always have lint stuck to it along with being oddly shaped since Oscar sat or slept on it. The kids always chewed it anyway.

Oscar liked hanging around the downtown Greenville area, and one could always find him since he stood out like a hair in milk. It would be a hundred degrees outside and Oscar would still be wearing that wool coat. Oscar wasn't the type of man who appeared to have a lot of friends, but everyone in the city knew him. Nobody messed with Oscar.

Kevin was used to seeing Oscar all over town, sitting outside a movie theater or at the corner booth at Tony's Ice Cream. His most popular hangout was Doug's Bicycle Shop, where Kevin had first met him. The owner of the shop would let Oscar come in to hang around and tell a few jokes to the customers. The jokes weren't always funny but people liked Oscar telling them.

In the last few months, Oscar had started selling a street paper he helped get started in Greenville called *StreetSounds*. Published monthly, every copy sold helped provide income for the homeless or formerly homeless as well as informing the public about their needs.

Kevin thought of the contrast between his life and Oscar's. Kevin had a family, a home, an office, and a job. All the things that a man seemed to need. But Oscar seemed not to be bothered by the fact that he didn't have those things.

Maybe because Oscar has friends and a community and an unwavering attitude of optimism.

He didn't know if Oscar was a man of faith, but he wouldn't doubt it.

What I wouldn't give to have the attitude of Oscar. Someone still motivated enough to help get a thing like StreetSounds *started in a city like Greenville.*

Sometimes something as simple as a paper costing a buck could be the spark of something else. Something bigger and more profound.

A simple and sweet thing called hope.

Maybe Kevin would go out and pick Oscar's brain. Perhaps Oscar would have a slogan that wouldn't be corny like the motivational posters or cynical like the ones from the comedy Web site. Some word of wisdom he lived by.

Maybe he and Oscar could go into business and sell Oscarisms. For a buck and a quarter, cheaper than getting your tire patched up at Doug's Bicycle Shop.

Kevin decided to get up and get out of his office. He wasn't accomplishing much except worrying and wondering. He had gotten nowhere trying to drum up new business. Everybody started shutting down when December 1 hit the calendar books.

There had to be something else he could do.

Then he thought of the gifts he still needed to get for the boy named Thomas.

That would be a perfect use of time.

*

Kevin was still thinking about Oscar when he picked out the Nike basketball shoes. He wanted to go all out, not to just go halfway with this gift.

Yeah, I'm losing my company soon, but I haven't lost it yet, and I still have credit, so lay off, conscience.

He had never worn Nike Air Jordans, so he wondered if they were really truly *that* great of a basketball shoe. But since the kid was asking for a Bulls jersey, how could he go with something else? He wasn't going to get anything with the name Kobe or LeBron on it. No way.

As he started to head toward the register carrying the first pair of shoes he'd bought in a year, ones that he wasn't even going to wear, Kevin heard his name called out. He turned and saw Bruce Helton walking toward him.

"Hey man," Kevin said.

Bruce was a former youth pastor at their church who had recently become an associate pastor of something-or-other.

Maybe you'd remember if you, oh, ever went to church.

Close to Kevin's age, he had worked with Precision a couple of years ago on a project for the church. They had done a few lunches and had talked about getting the families together one day. But life was full of a lot of "one day"s.

"How's Jenny doing?"

"Oh, she's hanging in there. Getting more uncomfortable with each passing day."

He thought of mentioning the most recent doctor's visit, but that was a lot of information for a random meeting at a sporting-goods store.

"And when's the official date again?"

"Well, technically forty weeks would get us to the middle of February, but doctors say it'll probably be sooner."

"Wow. Twins. So you planning a little early to start them playing ball?"

For a second Kevin didn't get his reference, then noticed the shoes in his hands. He thought about telling Bruce about the Angel Tree he and Jenny had signed up for, but then thought that might be bragging.

You know I rarely come to church and rarely give to the church but hey, look at these awesome shoes I'm donating to a kid I don't even know.

"Yeah," Kevin said, trying to shut up his wandering thoughts. "I bought a pair of football cleats for the other. Hedging my bets."

As they spoke, Kevin kept waiting and wondering when he'd hear it, the inevitable "Haven't seen you guys around for a while." But it never came. Bruce acted like it was just yesterday when they were working on the project and going to lunch and comparing notes about their families.

"Remember that missions trip I took to Ethiopia a few years ago?" Bruce asked.

The one I first said I was going on too?

"Yeah, I remember," Kevin said.

"Heading back there next year."

Again, Kevin waited to hear it. The question. The invitation.

I got twins arriving and a company sinking. I can't go anywhere.

"I've been thinking of calling you about it," Bruce said.

Here it comes.

"I think I have a project that I could really use your team on. It's a movie."

Kevin's heart stopped like a rattle finally dropping. He not only felt stupid but also ashamed. His face grew hot and he was sure he was blushing.

"Cool—a movie you guys are doing?"

"Yeah, something like that. Any chance we can do lunch again soon? Would love to work together again."

Work. Again.

"That'd be great," Kevin said. "Just e-mail me. Or contact me through Facebook."

"I keep up-to-date on your life through it."

"I'm sure we'll be posting a thousand photos once those babies come."

After saying good-bye to the pastor, Kevin found his mind racing. It had been a while since he'd seen Bruce. Now there was a slight possibility of work.

And yet another reason for me to stop playing around and go back to church.

As he started up the car, he glanced at the bag that contained the shoe box and the very expensive shoes inside of it.

Maybe those shoes were worth it. Just maybe.

It's Bad When

The two cribs stood side by side where his desk used to be. The room used to be his home office, and it was officially where Precision Design started when Kevin left the corporate world. They'd pretty much finished the nursery, with Jenny's parents helping tremendously. But there was still one more thing to add to the room.

Just yesterday they had decided on the names for the boys. Mark and Benjamin. Baby A was Mark, and Baby B was fittingly Benjamin. To celebrate, Jenny had run out and bought capital letters *M* and *B* that could go on the wall right above each crib. She had wanted Kevin to hang them right away, but he had paused, telling her it might be better to wait until her father could do it. He was a perfectionist and usually did a better job.

That was only an excuse, however.

There's another reason you don't want to put those letters on the wall, isn't there?

It was late at night and the one lamp on the children's dresser was on. He was sitting in Jenny's rocking chair, the place she'd spent so much time nursing Gregory after he was born. He tried to picture both of the babies in this room but he just couldn't.

You just don't want to.

The door gently swept open and Jenny came into the room.

"Whatcha doing?" she asked.

He shook his head casually, shrugging. "Nothing. Just thinking."

"About the twins?"

"About everything," he said.

She stayed by the door for the moment, waiting to see if he wanted to talk. Jenny knew there were many times he did want to talk and other times he didn't want to talk, or be chipper, or share his thoughts.

"You know what I don't get about myself?" he asked.

"What?"

She walked into the room and leaned against the closest crib.

"Here—sit," he said, standing.

"No, it's fine."

"Come on. You'll be in that chair pretty soon."

"Yeah, I know," Jenny said, taking his advice and resting on the chair.

For a moment Kevin looked at the crib that they had designated for Baby B. For Benjamin. For the baby that would have the nice fat *B* hanging on the wall above him.

"Sometimes I wonder why it's so difficult for me to be positive."

"About Benjamin?"

"Yeah. And about—about everything."

"That's just your nature."

He looked over at her and nodded. "Have I always been like that?"

"Think so."

"I just wonder why it's so much easier to worry than it is to hope," Kevin said.

He looked at the blue *B* resting against the crib at his feet.

"So you are worried," Jenny said.

No, not worried exactly. More like terrified.

"I'm just thinking about everything. Like what will happen if this happens or if this doesn't happen."

"I know," Jenny said. "I'm the same way."

"I'm sorry," he said, not looking at her when he said it but looking at the bedding in the crib.

"About what?"

"About—about the company. That this had to happen at this moment—"

"Kev."

"What?"

"Stop."

He looked at her and knew she was right. He was panicking, feeling overwhelmed.

"It's going to be okay," she said in her calm and soft voice.

"You know it's bad when a hormonal mother expecting twins tells you to stay calm."

She laughed. "I didn't say 'stay calm.' I just said things are going to be okay."

"I know."

"I really believe that. I really believe God's going to take care of us. I have to or else I just worry about it all day long."

Like I do, huh?

"Just the timing of everything happening with Precision—"

"Is meant to be," she finished.

He smiled and walked over to her, kissing her on the forehead and then helping her stand.

"I'm tired," she said. "And you look beat. You should come to bed."

"It's bad when a tired mother of twins tells you that you look beat."

"Stop with this 'It's bad when' stuff. Stop thinking bad thoughts."

It's easy for you to say.

"Don't worry, okay?" she added. "Things are going to be fine."

Jenny left him alone again. The room was quiet. He tried imagining the two of them in here, each holding a baby, Gregory running around grabbing pacifiers and wipes and diapers and burp cloths. He thought of little round cheeks smiling up at him with a smile that didn't know worry or fear but simply wanted to be by Mommy or Daddy.

For a second he felt as if his heart were suspended in air in the middle of this room.

Lord, please be with those boys.

It'd been so long since he sat in silence and prayed. So long.

Kevin hoped that God didn't keep track of how long it'd been.

A Common Bond

Thomas lay in bed unable to sleep. All he could think of was the game. It had been a close one against Wake Forest, a team the Tarheels should've beaten. Should've blown out. But they weren't sharp, not tonight.

Games like this one got him fired up to go and play. He wanted to be the guy holding the ball with ten seconds left, their team down by two.

He wanted to be the one to drain that three-point shot.

His mind raced, picturing the scene, imagining the dream.

And then suddenly he realized that for the first time in some time, he missed his father.

Sure, the guy was mean. Didn't matter if he was drinking or not, his father was never warm and cuddly. But he loved sports and he especially loved the University of North Carolina. His father used to play point guard during high school and college, so his favorite thing to do was sit back in his chair, yell at the screen and make calls, drinking beer and usually cheering since the Tarheels were so good.

It just wasn't the same watching them on the small television in this trailer with the Christmas tree that still needed to be decorated.

Thomas knew why.

It wasn't because of the size of the television or the fuzziness of the reception or the fact that Mom and Sara were not interested in the game.

It was because his father wasn't there.

The season had just started and that was when Thomas realized that the person who sat beside him watching the games hadn't been around for quite some time.

It was the same person who once played, the same person who always encouraged Thomas in his playing.

"You can dribble around him because you're faster than he is," Dad would tell him after watching him during a game. "You can drain that shot because you're taller than him."

It was a shared bond. It was only now that Thomas realized how much it meant to him. Not to his father, but to him.

Watching the game by himself was just that—it was always better to share the experience.

Thomas realized that his father didn't just laugh and yell and curse and cheer along with the Tarheels. He encouraged and educated his son during the games too.

He wouldn't believe it if I told him I wasn't playing because of some school technicality. He'd be angry.

Sometimes he wondered if he'd ever see his dad again, and what he would say if he did.

Tonight, Thomas wished and hoped he could see his father again. He needed to see him again.

Maybe he was thinking about Dad because of the other

evening driving home from Uncle Jesse's and what Mom had said.

"Don't hate your father. We're all sinful and God is working in all of us. You, me, Sara, your father."

Working in all of us.

Thomas wondered if God was really working in his father. Would they ever know? All he could do was pray for him.

I wonder if he's in his chair half passed out from drinking, thinking about the game. Or maybe, just maybe, thinking about his son.

A Tiny Fraction of Hope

It was Sunday but so far Lynn hadn't had much rest and she certainly hadn't seen much of the Lord. It was late at night and the kids had gone to bed. She sat on her couch, too wired to watch television or read a book or do anything other than look through the Help Wanted ads again. As if they might have been magically updated in the newspaper like they were on the Internet.

This lasted only a few minutes until her tired eyes closed and her frustration boiled over.

This was as good a time as any to have a little conversation. One she'd been putting off for a while.

"Why are you doing this?"

She was angry at Him and she wanted an answer. She needed an answer.

But Lynn had a feeling an answer wasn't going to come.

"I just wanna know what I did to deserve this. What did I do?"

He didn't say anything.

He'd always been quiet, ever since she'd come to know Him. And especially since everything started going downhill with Daryl.

"I can keep askin', can't I?"

Her voice echoed off the tin walls. A tin voice in a tin house.

"I'm not going to stop askin'."

Maybe He knew that.

It wasn't going to change His mind.

"I'm not talking about going to Nashville and singin'. I'm not talking about those dreams I used to have. I'm talking about livin'. I'm talking about trying to just *live.* Is that too much to ask? Is it?"

Nothing.

Nothing but silence.

Silence and that stark naked Christmas tree just sitting there in the corner. Sitting and staring at her.

"Why won't you talk to me? Why won't you tell me? I just want one answer. I just want something. I want to see a little tiny fraction of hope in this place. In my life. In our lives."

Nothing.

"Please."

Still nothing.

"If I gotta get on my knees, I will. Lord, You know I'll do it."

And that was exactly what she did.

She continued talking to Him, even though it sure seemed as though He wasn't listening.

But Lynn wasn't giving up and she wasn't letting go.

God heard her, and she knew that.

Even if He wasn't answering, He heard her.

And maybe—just please, God, maybe—He would answer one of these prayers and let a door open and let hope seep on in.

As Poor as I Am

Monday morning brought the reality of going to school again. The reality of Vic and the basketball team he continued not to be a part of. The reality of the whole Facebook thing that Thomas had been able to sorta forget over the weekend. The reality that Christmas was twenty days away.

Regardless of whether he actually received the presents he'd listed for the Angel Tree program, Thomas knew that he was going to get one very big and very wonderful present soon: time off from school. A couple weeks, in fact. And that would give him more time to try to find a job, something he'd been working hard at ever since Mom lost hers.

If only I can make it through the next two weeks.

Since discovering the Facebook thing, he'd tried to shrug it off. But that just wasn't working. He might act cool and carefree, but he was anything but. All he wanted was the school year to be over. He wanted to wake up and find himself twenty-four years old living in a new state with a new life.

Instead, he found himself approached by a familiar face and voice in the silence of his bedroom.

"Whatcha doing?"

Sara usually didn't bother him in the mornings unless she wanted something. And usually when she wanted something, he didn't have it to give to her. It was a very simple relationship, one that involved him saying "Can't help you out" over and over.

"Please tell me it snowed a foot and we're having a snow day," Thomas said to her.

"I don't think it's ever snowed a foot around here."

Sara might not have been a lot of things, but she *was* smart. And like her brother she could be a bit of a smart aleck.

He still had wet hair from the shower. "What do you want?"

She shrugged in a way that said she wasn't going anywhere.

"What?" he asked again.

"I saw."

"You saw what?"

"I saw—the Web site. The Facebook page."

"Who told you?"

"Pretty much everyone."

"Pretty lame, isn't it?"

She shook her head as she glanced his way.

"So, what is it, then?"

"Aren't you going to get it taken down?"

"By who? The Facebook police?" Thomas picked up his backpack that had only one good strap left on it.

"Did you do *anything*?" his sister asked.

"The bus is going to come soon."

She blocked the door, so he paused, not wanting to make a bigger deal out of this.

"Don't worry," he said. "The whole thing is stupid."

This was not only irritating, now it was really angering him. For a moment he thought of the things he wanted to tell his sister, but then as he looked at her he could tell she was starting to cry.

"Why're you doing that?" Thomas asked.

She shook her head and looked down. Thick hair hid her face from him.

"Sara?" He faced her so she would look at him.

"What?"

"Why are you upset?"

"I'm not."

Girls.

"What is it, then?"

"It's embarrassing."

Thomas couldn't say anything to his sister. Yeah, it was embarrassing. But he'd never really realized anybody but him was actually being embarrassed. Then it hit him.

She's part of my family. She's just as poor as I am.

"It's going to be gone soon," he told her.

"I just don't get it."

"What?"

"Why don't you stick up for yourself?"

She looked at him.

"Look—it's really just—"

But Sara was already gone.

*

He had asked Carlos to borrow his laptop again during lunch. Just like last time, he didn't want to do this on one of the computers in the middle of the computer lab where others could see. He wanted to do this in the back of the library where nobody would bother him.

As Thomas logged onto his Facebook page, the one that never had much of anything on it, he thought of Sara.

Why don't you stick up for yourself?

He'd thought all morning about the page and about Vic and about why he would do something like he'd done. But then something shifted inside of him. He wasn't sure why or for what exact reason. Maybe it came from what was going on with Mom, what was happening to them, the idea behind the gifts for the Angel Tree. And right then and there he just knew. As with other ideas he'd had, Thomas knew it the moment the idea came to him. He wasn't trying to be anything he wasn't. It just felt like a pretty cool idea and he thought, *Why not?* What was the worst thing to happen?

It didn't take him long to reach the page again that showed that ugly picture of him.

Feed the Hungry

He stared at it for another moment and started to have second thoughts.

Do it now or you'll never do it.

Thomas clicked on the "Like" button.

As he did, he could feel the tingles on his body.

The picture of him in his profile was over a year old, but it still looked like him. People would probably do a double take when they saw that he'd joined this page.

They might start thinking it's a joke or something.

He was going to do more than simply join the page, however. On the main screen, where comments from students ranged from "Who is this guy?" to "Hilarious," Thomas wrote a message to all 145 people who liked the page.

> Want to really "Feed the Hungry"? Want to really do some good this Christmas?
>
> Get a gift for someone in need.
>
> Someone REALLY in need. Not just a high school student who doesn't have much of a wardrobe. From now until Christmas break, all donations can be brought to locker #1700. I'm leaving my locker unlocked for all gifts. I'll then bring them to the Salvation Army the week before Christmas.
>
> Let's do something good. As a school.

He posted the comment and then shut off the laptop.

There.

A part of him wondered if someone would do something to his locker, but then again, he didn't have anything to steal. Now he'd just wait and see what his fellow students were really, truly about. Not Vic, but the rest of the school.

He was going to tell Carlos and his buddies about the page—to join it and the cause. And maybe, just maybe . . .

Opportunities

Nobody could ever criticize Kevin for not trying, for not working hard enough. He realized that sometimes trying and working weren't enough, that so often the great successes in life, whether they were in business or the arts, ended up arriving because of a combination of skill and timing and luck. Being at the right place at the right time with the right idea. That didn't discourage him, however, not even after the roadblock that had recently come up that could really truly be a dead end.

I can still be at the right place at the right time.

So every day, he started out updating his to-do list, making a list of potential opportunities and projects, marking whom to reach out to and whom to connect with. He was using the Internet to his advantage, using those pesky social networks to connect.

He'd usually be able to get in an hour and a half of work before reaching the office. But this morning, he had a couple of meetings at Starbucks. The first one was to connect and to receive some much-needed encouragement. The second one—well, that was probably to say good-bye.

*

"So what exactly are you going to do?"

Kevin had spent the last half hour sharing with Matt Zay everything that was going on with Precision. After Kevin told Matt about losing his biggest client, his old friend from his old church wanted to know how Kevin planned on supporting his family. "I was hoping to come work for you," Kevin joked.

Matt worked with foster kids, and both of them knew that it was a tough job that didn't pay well. "I'll take you anytime."

"I'm trying everything I can. Every day I contact about ten people I've worked with. But—the timing really bites, you know. Things start to shut down near the middle of December. I only have a good week left before things are going to get too tight."

Before the slack in the noose gives and I can't breathe.

Matt sipped his coffee and crossed a leg. "Have you tried the publisher you used to work for?"

"Autumn House? Not yet."

"How'd you leave things with them?"

"They had to get a restraining order against me, but you know—other than that, all things were good. No—everything was fine. I could see going back there too. Who knows? There've been times the last few years with Precision that I thought, 'Man, wouldn't it be nice to have someone else worry about paying the bills and the benefits and all that?' But I've invested everything in the company. And I mean *everything*."

"You're like the third guy I've talked to in the last month who's looking for a job."

Kevin shook his head. "I'm looking to save mine. There's a difference."

"Yeah, guess you're right. With the twins coming, it's smart to be prepared."

He couldn't help but laugh at Matt's comment. Matt was a good guy with an optimistic heart and an encouraging attitude. They'd lost touch since Kevin and Jenny switched churches after Gregory was born.

"I would have been more prepared if I'd had a clue they weren't going to re-sign with us," Kevin said. "But it just seems each year gets busier and busier."

"Yeah, well, maybe that's prepared you well. Since you're about ready to become *extremely* busy."

"What if I grew my hair long and my beard out and I became Mr. Mom? Remember that movie?"

"Does that include nursing?"

"I can give it a try."

It was good to laugh and to be able to tell Matt some of what he was dealing with. Most of the conversations he had recently were short and sweet—conversations about working together and doing business and developing projects and ideas. Most of the people he spoke with sounded enthusiastic, but they were merely blowing smoke. Matt didn't have to. He could simply listen and ask Kevin how he felt and not make any promises, or fill him with false hope.

It felt good to have someone he could confide in without the need of any kind of response. Sometimes simply sharing what was happening was enough to give him some peace of mind.

*

As his first casual meeting morphed into a second business meeting, Kevin soon found his suspicions correct.

"I'm sorry I have to do this."

Kevin nodded and took a sip of cold coffee and then took in the moment. *Shouldn't I be the one letting him go?*

But instead, Zack, his most talented and hardworking designer, was leaving him.

As if he didn't have enough things to worry about.

But this could be a blessing in disguise. Now I don't have to worry about Zack finding a job.

But Zack was always going to find another job. Kevin had already encouraged two of the designers, Pete and recently hired Samantha, to start looking around at prospects. But he hadn't been able to encourage Zack to do the same.

Because you're stubborn and you want to always do things your way.

"I know that Pete and Sam have started sending out résumés."

Kevin couldn't really say much except "Yeah."

"Landmark is going to pay me a lot more. The benefits are better too. I just had to . . ."

Again, the nod and the sip.

Ten years of hard work, scattered on this table like pieces of a jigsaw puzzle that I have no time to put together.

"There's not a lot I can say," Kevin said. "I mean, I don't want you to go. But I have no idea—I can't promise any of you anything."

"Yeah, I know. I just—I can't afford to be out of work."

And why's that? Need to keep making payments on that sporty new SUV you just got?

The guy was twenty-five, Kevin reminded himself. *Give him a break.*

He'd worked hard at making Precision the kind of company where young guys like Zack, who drove sporty VW SUVs and wore cool glasses and did amazing, irreplaceable work, would want to work.

"If things were different, I'd make a counteroffer," Kevin said.

"I know."

"*When* things get a little more stable, I'll be calling you. Okay?"

Kevin glanced at the late-morning sun spilling into the Starbucks and the shadow from an armchair reaching out and touching his feet. The day had started so brightly, with so many opportunities and ideas. Now it felt like someone was running away with all of them.

Staring at the guy across the table, he knew that Zack really was irreplaceable.

"So when do you start the new job?" Kevin asked.

"First of January."

"Ouch."

"I know, man. I'm sorry."

He recalled the last time they were in this Starbucks. Kevin had talked to Zack about how things were going to be when the twins came, about the adjustment and how that might mean more responsibilities for his up-and-coming designer.

Every man, woman, and child for himself.

Kevin had tried to make the point that more responsibilities meant more opportunities for Zack.

There it was again. That word. That wonderful little word that felt more elusive with each passing day.

Opportunities.

He couldn't really promise anything resembling an opportunity when he might not be able to pay rent next month and might have to let his employees all go.

"I don't want to bail on you like this. I just have to."

"You're not bailing. You're being responsible. You've got a lot going on, Zack."

"Maybe things will change."

"The door is always open," Kevin said. Then he couldn't resist adding, "If in fact there's a door to open. Maybe it'll just be the door to my van. The one my family will be living in down by the river."

Zack was always one to laugh at his jokes, funny or not.

Life was strange. You could see somebody every day for 95 percent of the year yet suddenly end up like this: sipping coffee, saying good-bye, knowing that you might never see each other again.

Kevin thought of this, then surprised himself when he said, "Don't let them make you into anything other than who you are, okay? Don't try to fit into some kind of box. You're really talented, and I'd hate to see you stop growing, stop using your creativity."

Zack looked concerned for a moment, like Kevin knew something he didn't. "Uh, thanks."

"Don't worry—they're probably going to help you be a better designer than I ever could as your boss. You got a crazy amount of talent, Zack. Don't let anybody keep you from using all of it."

Perhaps not too long ago, Kevin might have held back with the heartfelt speech simply because he might have thought it was uncool. But it didn't matter.

He was beginning to understand that life was a series of moments. It wasn't about thinking on the past or about speculating over the future. It was about the moment he was in right that very second.

"Thanks, man, that really means a lot."

There was so much more to do. So many more *opportunities* left to pursue. But for a few more moments Kevin shared one last coffee with Zack, trying to encourage him with his dreams.

He was trying to stay in the moment.

It was hard to do, but he managed.

If only he could do the same with everything else in his life.

The Note

His sister would be proud if she saw him now.

Thomas walked toward the locker where he hoped Vic would be. In his hand he held the most recent and hopefully *last* joke that Vic would be playing on him. Enough was enough and jokes were jokes. Thomas was done with it all. It was one thing with the stupid Facebook page that he was trying to do something good with. But now, a day later, Vic was still tormenting him. He was mocking him with something that would never happen, that *could* never happen.

Enough bullying.

Vic was there all right, in his school sweats, looking as if he was ready to start practice.

If Thomas stopped now, he knew he wouldn't go through with it. So he kept going and nearly plowed right into an unsuspecting Vic, who was getting a book out of his locker.

Thomas threw the note into the locker as if it were a piece of trash. "Good one, man," he called out.

Vic turned around and looked at him.

For a moment there was this look of disbelief on the guy's face.

I look that unconvincing, huh?

Vic spit out a curse word and turned around, ignoring him.

"I mean it, man. I'm serious."

Vic picked up the note and turned around as he slowly opened it.

"What do you think you're doing?"

"Why don't you lay off me?"

Vic read the note for a minute, then looked at Thomas, then looked back at the note.

"You're a redneck fool, you know that?" Vic said.

"Takes one to know one," Thomas said, suddenly feeling as if he were in third grade.

A couple of Vic's friends came up near the locker to observe a potential fight.

"What is your deal, boy?" Vic asked.

"I'm sick of jokes like that."

"Like your Facebook page?" Vic sneered at him, causing the guys who had just walked up to snicker.

"Yeah, well, maybe you oughta take a look at that page now," Thomas said.

"And why's that?"

Thomas ignored his question. "What'd I ever do to you? Huh? Tell me."

"I'm tellin' you that you wave that little bony finger in front of my face ever, and I mean *ever* again, I'm going to break it in so many pieces that you'll never be able to put it back together."

Control. Breathe. Don't run. Don't pass out.

"So I beat you in a game. Are you ever going to get over it?"

Vic tossed the note to the floor in front of Thomas.

"I'll tell you this—if I wasn't being watched like a hawk, I'd make you eat that stupid letter. But I want to play ball for my school. Got that? I get to play ball for my school."

"Just give me time," Thomas said.

"Time before what?"

"You might end up watching me play while you sit."

The look on the bully's face revealed that Thomas wasn't that far off with the comment. Vic had seen enough. Before he walked away, he added, "And look—if I wanted to play tricks with your head, I'd use someone a lot more believable than Cass to do it with. I'm not the only one who thinks you're a mutant."

With that Vic left, leaving Thomas to realize that the letter really, truly was from Cass.

I didn't believe it despite what Carlos had said.

He picked up the letter that suddenly wasn't a mocking taunt from a stupid bully but rather a nice note from a girl who obviously was interested in him.

He glanced around the hallway to see if anybody else watched him.

Suddenly Thomas felt more fear than he had in going to confront Vic.

A Handshake

Kevin could hear the steady ticking this Thursday evening even though there wasn't a single clock in his office that could be seen. The minutes were passing and they'd soon be gone just like he would be.

He'd called Jenny an hour ago telling her he was going to stay late, not to wait for him for dinner. He wanted to make sure she was set and asked if she needed anything. She was fine. Always fine. Uncomfortable but fine.

The office was empty when the last person left around five. There was still work that needed to be done, but not enough to really keep them here after hours. He was trying to douse the flames on this burning building. Maybe he could stop it, but it was already wreaking havoc, destroying everything in its path.

Is it really that bad, Kev?

He knew the unfortunate truth to that question. After looking at his bank accounts online, then going over the list of contacts that had been scratched out on his spiral-bound notebook where he kept important details, Kevin knew it really was that bad.

It was Friday and he'd gotten nowhere. There was a list of a dozen projects and clients that were all maybes. *Maybe we'll send you something. Maybe we'll do something in the new year. Maybe we'll throw you a bone*. But none of those maybes could make up for the no he heard from Silverschone.

He was tired of people hiding behind digital walls. Nobody shook hands anymore, or looked you in the eye. That was why he'd gone personally to see Dan at Silverschone, to be there face-to-face, to try to make them realize that Precision was more than just another business. There were people involved. Not just names and profiles and witty caricatures on Twitter. Everybody was LinkedIn but nobody really, truly connected.

He was currently linked in to the Web trying to search for something, anything, to jump-start his last-ditch efforts. Searching around for businesses that he had never worked for in the Greenville area that might be an ideal fit for his company. Looking at other agencies to get ideas. Yet too often, he found himself running in circles like a dog chasing after a bone he could never grab from his master.

He might end up joining the large percentage of unemployed doing the same exact thing he was doing. He wouldn't be officially there next week or next month—Precision still had some projects that would trickle in some money. But the staff and this building and all this wonderfully glorious potential—there was no maybe for that. It was gone and Kevin knew it.

Out of the thousand people who were "friends" on Facebook, Kevin was looking at a former colleague at Autumn House Publishers. It had been a while since they'd spoken, and Kevin was thinking about sending him a message.

Hi, friend, how are you? Long time no talk. How's life? And by the way, do you have any jobs you can spare?

He thought about it but never actually started the note. It felt too impersonal and too abrupt and frankly too desperate.

Well, don't want to burst your bubble, Kev, but you are a little desperate, you know?

He found a link that sent him to a local news piece, highlighting a college student who was giving up his next semester at Clemson in order to walk for the homeless for six months. The reporter talked about how this kid had been impacted after spending a night working at a food kitchen in downtown Greenville. The student said that after seeing homelessness for the first time, he decided he wanted to do something more than spend a couple hours doing something anybody could do in their sleep.

Maybe I'll do the same. I'll walk for a cause and get publicity and then out of that I'll end up finding all these doors opening.

Kevin clicked off the link and felt ashamed at the thought. Greenville didn't exactly have an overwhelming homeless problem, but he knew that there were other charities he could do something like this for. It had been a long time since he'd done anything for charity. It had been a long time since he'd done much of anything except try to build this company into something profitable and exciting.

Maybe he's got the whole thing right, Kevin thought about the college kid.

Instead of focusing on school and career and the future, this kid was doing something tangible and real and meaningful. For people who didn't have anything. Not just looking for jobs, but looking for a life.

Kevin thought about the Angel Tree program. He quickly shut off his computer as well as the melancholy thoughts and decided to head to the Apple Store on the way home. He still needed to get "Thomas" an iPod. Maybe he would browse for a few minutes and see all the toys he'd love to write down on an angel ornament one day too.

*

He was almost out of the store—seconds away from opening the glass door and exiting—when he glanced over and saw Amanda. At first, Kevin paused, thinking that he was not really seeing the woman. But a face that recognized him and smiled with surprise confirmed it.

"Kevin—Kevin Morrell?"

Amanda Lake walked over and gave him a big hug. An energetic beam of a smile lit up her pretty face.

"What are you doing around here?" Kevin asked. "I thought you guys moved to Texas."

"We're in Nashvegas now. Gotta love it, huh? We're visiting my parents for a couple of weeks before we head to Massachusetts to spend Christmas with the in-laws."

Amanda looked tanned and toned and still young, even though they were the same age. Life was definitely treating her well, Kevin thought.

"You guys are expecting, right?" Amanda asked with a zeal that seemed heartfelt and real.

"Yeah. Couple more months. Hopefully."

"Twins, right?"

"How'd you know that?" Kevin asked.

"Jenny's Facebook page."

"Oh, yeah."

For a few moments Kevin talked about how Jenny was doing and the usual stuff. He didn't tell Amanda that he was a few steps away from freaking out.

"You still at the same company?" Kevin asked.

"No, thankfully. Can you believe this? The company I was working at in Texas was the wrong fit. A lot of money but just—totally wrong. And we'd just moved out there, you know. A little scary with the kids and everything. But then I got with Texan Resort in Grapevine. It's the sister hotel to the Opryland. What—a—blessing. That was a total miracle, to say the least."

Kevin nodded, totally curious, especially about the miracle part. He'd met Amanda while working at Autumn House fifteen years ago. Amanda had worked for a major ad agency in Greenville and the two had crossed paths on a couple of projects. Kevin, of course, had envied the cool vibe and personality of Amanda's agency. He would often find himself picking her brain to see how things were done and why they were done that particular way whenever Amanda came to meet with the staff at the publisher. A lot of the structure and style that had gone into Precision, now a major competitor to Amanda's former agency, had come from those conversations.

"You still working in publicity?"

Amanda nodded. "Yeah—and this is the crazy thing. I was with the Texan Resort for like a month and then they brought me to the headquarters. So just like that, we ended up moving to Nashville."

"Closer to your parents," Kevin said.

"Yeah. Texas was fine but—it was Texas, you know? These guys—I mean, I'm telling you, they're incredible to work for. And ever since the flood in Nashville, they've been working hard to get the word out that they're still around and still in business."

He grinned at her. "You're pretty good at getting the word out."

"Always."

When she asked how things were going with Precision, he simply downplayed everything. Kevin couldn't tell Amanda what was really going on, not here in the Apple Store with so many people around them.

"It's so good running into you," Amanda said. "Tell Jenny I said hi and please keep me in the loop on how things go with the twins."

"Yeah, certainly."

Amanda gave him another hug before Kevin walked out the doors.

Maybe there were few handshakes these days. But sometimes there were hugs.

Kevin made a note to himself that he planned on following up with Amanda. Very soon. Maybe, just maybe, there could be a chance to work with her again and make some inroads with a company like Gaylord Hotels.

He glanced down at the bag he was carrying and suddenly felt a wave of goose bumps. He paused and looked around. Just for a moment. He half expected Christmas music to be playing and snow to start falling. It was weird, but he felt like things were strangely being orchestrated by someone.

Something So Cool

It was only a matter of time before Thomas had the confrontation. It made him think of the classic movie *High Noon* that he'd watched once with his father. But unlike Gary Cooper he wasn't armed and wasn't ready and if he could he'd take the first train out of here. But Friday morning before first period, Thomas realized that it was finally time and he needed to stand strong.

"Hi, Thomas," Cass said to him as she walked up carrying a shopping bag in each hand. "Can I still give these to you?"

For the moment Thomas forgot what those bags were for. He forgot what was in them and why she was bringing them to him. For the moment he forgot pretty much everything except the golden-haired-cheerleader-babe who was finally coming up to him after the week he'd spent avoiding her since reading that letter.

"Or I can give them to someone else if your locker's already completely full," she said with an amused, confident look on her face.

"No, it's fine, really," Thomas said, opening his locker and then seeing an avalanche of stuff falling out of it.

With his ankles buried in clothes, blankets, a bag full of canned goods, a video game, another bag tied at the top, Kevin could feel his face warming to a nice red glow. He laughed as he tried to take the bags out of Cass's hands.

"Here," she said, setting the bags on the floor and stooping to help him pick up everything. "Is this everything you've gotten this week?"

He shook his head, back in reality. "This is everything I've gotten this morning."

"Are you kidding?"

"No." Kevin let out a nervous chuckle. "It's been kinda crazy."

"I think it's kinda awesome."

"Yeah, that too."

"So where is everything going?"

"Leonard's letting me store it in a closet."

Cass had both arms full. "Who's Leonard?"

"The janitor."

"Oh, yeah," she said.

For a moment he didn't know whether to take the stuff from her or if she was going to put it back in the locker.

"Want to show me the magical closet?" Cass asked.

"Oh, yeah, sure, thanks."

He was stammering. Surely she was going to figure out that this was not the guy she'd written that nice letter to. That guy was the new guy, the mystery guy, the guy full of intrigue. Standing before her was a dork named Thomas.

"Want to show me now?"

Thomas nodded, apologized, then felt his face turn red

again. As he walked, wondering what she might be thinking as she followed him, he was surprised when she came out with the obvious.

"So did you get my letter?"

He would have loved to have some kind of clever comeback. But "Yeah" was the only thing he could think to say.

"Stupid, huh?"

Thomas shook his head, his hands loaded down.

"I just thought it might be nice—to show you that not all people around here are total morons. I didn't have an e-mail or phone number."

"Thanks. I just didn't know what—"

"It's fine," she said. "Don't worry about it."

Before getting to the closet where several days' worth of items were collected to give to the homeless, Cass said, "Hey Thomas?" in a way that made him stop. He wondered if something was wrong.

"I think it's really amazing what you did. I don't think I would've done something so cool."

He shrugged, uncomfortable with the compliment and *really* uncomfortable that it came from Cass.

"Confirms what I thought when I wrote the letter," she continued.

"What's that?" he managed to say. Or more like he had to say.

But Cass only smiled this time.

Stripped and Left Barren

It was her fourth interview in three days, and this one was probably the worst. The guy had spent the time running his eyes up and down her body while ignoring half the things she said. Partway through, Lynn had realized that even if he offered her more money than she expected, she would rather live on the streets than work for him. When he said he'd give her a call, his tone told her it might not actually be to offer her a job but for something else.

The job had been all wrong for her anyway. It was a basic receptionist job, but she didn't have the right experience. Waiting tables was something she could do. Answering phones was something she could do as well. But when he started talking about the computer and running Microsoft Excel and making spreadsheets—that was when she was lost. It was embarrassing to admit, but she'd never spent much time on computers. She couldn't really type. As he talked about her sending e-mails and typing letters, she had known that this wouldn't be the right fit.

And obviously he could get someone else who could serve as eye candy as well as work on the computer.

As Lynn walked down the street, she found it odd to think of herself as attractive. Sure, she had dressed up as best she could for the interview, but she hadn't thought of herself as pretty since before she became a mother. When she and Daryl met, during those early days of dating, he'd made her feel like the most beautiful girl in the world. *The strains of motherhood have a way of aging a person,* she thought.

Now whenever guys looked, and more often they didn't, she just assumed they were the kind who looked at any living and breathing woman between ages fifteen and fifty.

Sometimes, in the stillness of her thoughts, she wished she could be beautiful again. It was something she would never admit or tell anybody, because dreams like that couldn't come true. One day she woke up and realized that the pretty young girl with all that potential had been replaced by a tired old mommy with all those wrinkles.

Before she got in her car, a voice startled her. It made her stop, not because it was sudden and out of the blue, but because she recognized it.

"Lynn."

For a moment she thought she was dreaming.

But there he was.

Standing on the corner in front of a store, looking like a beat-up road sign.

Daryl.

She froze for a moment, too scared to panic, too surprised to say anything.

"How are you?" he asked.

Everything in her suddenly became defensive.

You want to know how I am? Really? After all this time?

"How'd you find me?" she asked.

"It took some doing."

She barely recognized him. He looked thin, almost sick, but he also looked as if he'd tried to clean up. Showered, shaved, his hair slicked back.

Her husband, at least still officially, stood there on the sidewalk, trying to find the words.

He certainly knows the right word when he wants to hurt you.

Daryl wasn't the best when trying to do anything else.

"Have you seen the kids?" she said.

"No," Daryl said.

"I don't want any trouble."

"There ain't gonna be any. I promise, Lynn."

"You've promised that before."

"I know."

She looked around. It wasn't as if people she knew would see them. She had nobody. But she still had her dignity. That was one thing nobody was ever going to take from her. And she didn't care who was around—if Daryl tried to do anything, anything whatsoever, Lynn would make sure any passing soul around knew about it.

"I just wanna talk."

"We're talking," she said.

"Somewhere a little more private, you know?"

She looked in Daryl's eyes and saw it. Not the fiery anger or icy resolve. She saw the empty look, like a forest that had been stripped and left barren and bleak.

"Please, Lynn."

It didn't matter that she hadn't spoken with him in almost a year. She still loved the man, despite how little it seemed he loved her back.

*

A few moments later, they sat in a small diner. She watched him try to hide his shaking hand from her. But when he lifted the cup of coffee, it was visible to both of them.

"When was the last time you drank?"

"It's been a while."

"When?"

"Thanksgiving," his hollow voice said.

She knew, sitting this close to him, that he was telling the truth. His complexion and his weight and his whole demeanor said so. She knew Daryl and she also knew a lot about alcoholics.

"What happened on Thanksgiving?"

"Enough."

She didn't want to know. She would worry and want to make things right. But that was what she'd said good-bye to when she realized that she could never make things right—not their marriage, not his alcoholism or his abuse. When she saw that there were two bright shining suns that were being eclipsed by their father, every day and every night, and that she was helpless to fix it, she knew she had to go.

"Why are you here?" Lynn asked.

He nodded, as if to acknowledge that the question was legitimate. "I just want to know how you're doing."

"We're getting by."

"You look pretty."

She thought of telling him about the job interview but didn't. He didn't deserve to know.

"How are the kids?"

You don't have a right to ask about them.

But of course he had a right to ask. He would always be their father. In some ways, she was glad to hear him ask. It showed that he missed them, at least in his own way.

"They're fine."

"Is Tom playing ball?"

"Daryl—"

"Is he?"

"That the only thing that matters to you?"

He paused, looking at her. Normally Daryl had fight rising up inside of him and filling those eyes, but now the glance that she saw only looked empty. "I just—I'm just wondering."

"No. The truth is he couldn't try out for the team. Not this year. Going to a new school is hard enough. And in our circumstances, it's even harder. And the poor guy couldn't even do the thing he loves to do the most."

"Sounds like you're blaming me," Daryl said.

"You're darn right I'm blaming you."

That angry viper look filled his face for a moment, but this time it didn't last. It didn't have the fuel necessary to keep going. Daryl suddenly looked defeated again. Defeated and old.

So very old for a man still only in his thirties.

"I'm sorry, Lynn."

"For what?"

"For everything."

"We're not coming back home."

"I didn't come here to ask you that."

"Then why are you here?"

Daryl picked up the spoon and held it firmly as if he was trying to bend it. He glanced around the diner and then stared at her again.

"Christmas is just a little ways away. I just wanted to make sure you were all right."

"We're doing fine."

That face, so full, so sad, so scarred. He stared at her for a moment, apparently trying to figure out what to say next. Then he reached into his pocket and pulled out a folded envelope. He put it on the table and for a moment it just sat there.

"Take it," Daryl said. "It's yours. It's not much. You know I don't got a lot, but it's yours. Saved it up the last five months."

Lynn swallowed.

This was her answer to prayer? This?

For a moment she tried to tell herself that there was no way she was going to take charity from this man. No way.

You asked for something and God gave you something.

It took every amount of strength inside of her to simply move her hand across the table to pick up the envelope.

"It's seven hundred bucks," he said. "Not a lot, but you know . . ."

"Where'd you get it?"

He looked at her and then shook his head. "Aw, don't give me that."

They still talked like husbands and wives. Not needing to

say everything because they both knew what the other was thinking.

"You've never had seven extra dollars, much less seven hundred," she said.

"Just take it. And tell them—tell Thomas and Sara that I miss them. That I love them."

She squeezed her hands over the envelope. "I can't tell them that."

"Why not?"

Lynn gave her husband a look that she was used to giving him—the look an adult gives a child when they should know better. "I think you know why."

Telling them that Daddy misses and loves them will only make the situation worse.

"Are you ever coming back?"

She didn't say anything.

"I'm trying," he continued. "I'm trying to get things in order. Lord knows I'm trying."

"I asked you every day for years and you never listened. How am I supposed to believe you now?"

He nodded. He knew. The booze was just the match that lit the fire. His rage and his disregard for family—those weren't things he could just suddenly say "So sorry" about and then move on.

"I'm trying, Lynn," he said.

"You've been 'trying' your whole life."

He shook his head and then wiped the sweat off his forehead. "This is different."

She stopped herself from saying something else, something

defensive and hurtful. He seemed different. And he was acting different. And the money was certainly different.

Maybe he really, truly is trying.

"Then that's a start, right?" she said. "You take it one day at a time. Just like all of us."

"Can I see them?"

"No."

"They're my children too."

"Not anymore." She leaned over the table so he'd hear the words she was whispering very carefully. "You ignored them long enough. You promised and you ignored that promise. You promised and then you lied."

"I can change." Daryl sighed. "I'm working on it every day."

"Good for you," she told him. "But maybe that's not good enough for the rest of us."

With those words, she stood up and wished him well, then walked out on the street and climbed into her car to head back to her home and her children.

Nice on a Bumper Sticker

Kevin couldn't remember the last time he'd been at church. It had been a while. He probably should have been listening to the sermon, but he couldn't help thinking about Jenny, who was resting at home, or Gregory, who was playing in the nursery. He thought of Baby A and Baby B and wondered when he would finally start calling them Mark and Benjamin. He thought of Precision and his employees. That just brought him back around to thinking of Jenny and Gregory and the babies, especially little Baby B.

In the lobby just moments earlier, he'd encountered the same thing he always got from their friends who hadn't seen them for quite some time. Their comments echoed in the Grand Canyon of his mind:

"How are the babies doing?"

"How's Jenny doing?"

"Twins, huh? Boy, oh, boy."

"Do you have names picked out?"

"Enjoy that hair before it falls out."

"Get some rest now."

"Start planning on college. And money for bail."

Kevin laughed and made quips. He loved the word *quip* because it sounded a bit short and a bit cheap and that was exactly what his wisecracks were. They managed to keep everyone at ease and smiling instead of wondering when he was going to implode.

He thought of one of the many classic lines from *Jerry Maguire* and realized he could have easily said it to everyone around him. "Don't worry, I'm not gonna do what you all think I'm gonna do, which is, you know, FLIP OUT!"

So even though outwardly he was doing fine, he still sat with a thousand thoughts attacking him.

Soon enough they would be going to another doctor's visit.

Soon enough they would know a little more about Baby B.

In the meantime, as Jenny said time and time again, all they could do was continue to pray.

"Continuing *to pray" means that I've already been praying.*

It was maybe—no, not maybe but probably—a good thing to pray now that he was at church again. Ironically, as if Jenny had called the church to tell them he was coming, the pastor spoke on Matthew 6:25–34. The message was "Don't Worry, Be Happy." And while the text was supposed to be comforting and uplifting, Kevin found it distressing.

Yes, when placed on a scale of eternity, were these issues something to worry about? No.

But fear seemed to know his name and know it well. It had

breakfast with him and texted him throughout the day and liked to ride home with him in the evening. It hung around even when he tried his best to get rid of it and when he camouflaged it with witty quips.

"Don't worry about tomorrow, because tomorrow will worry for itself," the pastor said.

Yeah, and so will I.

He wondered what Jenny would have thought of the comment. She would have agreed and probably nudged him with a *See what I keep telling you?* She was so steady and stable. Even a hormonal Jenny with twins was still steady and stable. He was the hormonal one. He was the one who needed to breathe deeply in order to stop hyperventilating.

Maybe I'm going to need to be placed on bed rest.

"Who is your master?" the pastor asked everyone.

He said things like "Trust is born out of surrender."

So I haven't completely surrendered yet, have I?

The sermon outline in the bulletin highlighted key points:

God is faithful.

Kevin could accept that.

We are valuable.

He could accept that too.

God is our provider.

Ditto on that.

So then why was it so hard to let go and let God?

That's nice on a bumper sticker but doesn't really work too well when you're worrying about paying bills and the growth of a baby when you can't do diddly about either.

He could hear his father lecturing that this was a learning

experience. *Everything* was a learning experience according to Dad.

Thanks, Dad. Thanks for making me feel like I'm still thirteen.

"Worry is counterproductive."

Thanks, Pastor. Thanks for making me realize that I'm a failure.

He made a fist with one hand and squeezed it as hard as he could as his other hand concealed it.

I'm so weak.

Women were the stronger ones. Why else would God choose them to carry children inside them for nine months? Guys would break down and go ballistic. Guys just couldn't handle the pressure.

He sighed

It's so hard surrendering, God.

During the closing prayer, Kevin silently uttered his own. It was simple but sincere. It felt strange and a bit awkward to be knocking at the door of someone he hadn't visited for a long time.

"Help me, God. Help us. Help this—all of this. Just please help."

He believed that God heard him. But it was so hard to believe more than that.

Kevin knew that he could work extremely hard and do every single thing he could think of to make his business work. But it still might not.

The same applied to this.

He could pray without ceasing but still it was up to God. All he had to do now was to simply let go and believe.

But you haven't sweated a single solitary drop for your faith in a long time, have you, Kev? So what makes you think you have any right for those prayers to be heard?

As the benediction played and the congregation began to file out of church, Kevin knew he was terrified.

He'd spent so long working so hard. Yet he was beginning to realize that he'd been working for one person: himself.

Family Portrait

"*This kid is* going to love this. He's going to be blown away."

Kevin held the autographed Chicago Bulls jersey in his hands. Ray had come through big-time.

"I probably should do something noble like you with that Christmas tree program you're doing," Ray said as he opened a couple of beers and handed one to Kevin. In Ray's world, it was about who you knew and how much you spent on them.

"Angel Tree."

"Yeah, sure."

As he followed Ray downstairs into the basement game room with its flat-screen television, Kevin figured his friend would probably forget what kind of tree it was. Ray didn't have time or energy for details like that. He did, however, have time to focus on his Clemson Tigers or his golf game, which was easier to do now that he lived on a golf course. Or maybe the million-dollar mansion his family lived in.

It was a world that Kevin had always hoped to step into one day.

A world that suddenly feels empty and hollow.

Sipping his beer as he sat on maybe the most comfortable love seat ever—something he noted every time his rear touched the luxurious leather—Kevin thought about that wonderful myth, "He who dies with the most toys wins." It was a myth and everybody knew it, even those with the toys. It wasn't about dying with the most toys. It was about living and playing with them day after day after day.

No it's not, he reminded himself. *It's about being able to have toys to give away. Even Ray gets that.*

Ray wasn't a spiritual man but he was slowly coming around, and Kevin had done all he could by simply being there. Getting the Michael Jordan jersey was reciprocation in the only way Ray knew, through his connections and his cash.

Kevin thanked his friend again as Ray turned on the massive flat-screen television.

"She wants half of the house. Can you believe it?" Ray cursed louder than the announcers commenting through the megaspeakers surrounding them. "What's she want me to do? Get a chain saw and cut the thing in half?"

"What about the girls?"

"We'll both have custody. She knows how I feel about the girls. She's not taking them away from me."

The Sunday-night football game was on, yet Ray looked up at the ceiling.

"I worked my brains out to get this house, and a year after we move in, what does she do? I mean—you gotta just love it, huh?"

Kevin had learned that it was okay to just let his friend talk. He didn't want to be one of those who tried to bolster Ray's morale with platitudes. He didn't want to beat down Ray's wife either. He just listened and let Ray know he was listening.

"Sometimes, man, I just—I don't know." Ray finished his beer and shook his head. "I mean, life really doesn't make sense, does it?"

"No it doesn't."

"You know—you don't have to come around here all the time and listen to me whine."

"I don't mind as long as you give me beer," Kevin joked.

"I had no idea. I mean none. And then one day when I got back from a day of golfing in my backyard, she hits me with this. I mean, I think it would've been better if there'd been another guy or if I abused her or something. Not knowing is what kills me. Not having any idea is what gets me."

"Yeah."

"This place depresses me because she picked out most everything. Except this room, of course. This was mine."

The irony wasn't lost on Kevin, not in this playroom downstairs, not in this house.

He knew that wealth and possessions and security were all sometimes just empty rooms that swallowed up echoes. They were filler and padding.

"I think back to that little place we had when we were just married. But I realized that we weren't happy even back then. It'd be easy, you know, to think that we were living this tranquil life in that tiny apartment. But that's not true. I was crazy busy and Stef was miserable. I always thought the moment we could get ahead, I could be less busy and she would by happy. But that woman was born miserable. At least around me."

After a few minutes of watching the game, Ray stood up to get another beer.

"I'm good," Kevin said, his bottle still half full.

As he watched the game on an amazing television in an immaculate house, Kevin thought that life seemed to like to play tricks on you. That just when you thought you had it figured out, something bad inevitably happened.

We're all pieces of a broken puzzle. But we're not the ones who can put it back together.

He noticed the family portrait on the wall, then sighed.

God was trying to tell him something.

Kevin just hoped that he'd get it. Not just get it, but *do* something with it.

Better and Worse

Carlos was standing by Thomas's locker as he walked toward it after getting off the bus. It was a strange thing, having friends at school, Thomas thought. The bus ride didn't smell as bad as it used to. He didn't walk into this building feeling a wave of dread like some character in a zombie movie. He didn't wonder what the day would be like. Instead, he found himself smiling at the big guy who was waiting for him.

Life was better when there were people who actually waited for you.

"Dude—tell me you got online last night," Carlos said.

"I got online last night."

Carlos looked shocked. "For real?"

"No, man. I told you, we don't have Internet."

"Then you gotta see this. Here."

Carlos pulled out his phone and played with the display for a few moments. Then he showed Thomas.

For a minute Thomas didn't know exactly what he was supposed to be reacting to. There was the infamous Facebook page again.

"Yeah, what?"

"See that?" Carlos pointed.

"See what?"

"You got over eight hundred people who like this page."

"Really?"

"Totally. And you gotta read the comments. They're great."

"I'll check it out in the media center later."

As they were talking, a couple of girls walked up to them and gave Thomas some plastic bags.

"We went shopping at Target this weekend," one of the girls said. "The tags are still on the clothes."

"Hope this helps," the other girl said.

"Bye, Thomas," the first one called out before leaving.

Carlos just stood there, surprised, with a smile on his face.

"What are you going to do with all this stuff you're getting?"

"Salvation Army. This weekend sometime."

"Need any help carrying it all over?"

Thomas nodded, realizing he hadn't thought that far ahead. He was still trying to find a job, still trying to find some ways to help Mom. The whole Facebook thing had started as a nice idea—kinda like a few other ideas he'd recently gotten—but that nice idea was starting to explode. In a good way.

"One final thing."

"Yeah?" Thomas said, opening his locker and seeing more items filling it.

"Did you hear about Vic?"

What now?

"No," Thomas said as he shut the locker door. He needed

to get to his first class on time. Every day last week he'd been late. Late for a cause, but still late.

"Vic got suspended for the prank he pulled. He's gone until the new year. Heard about it because he couldn't play ball this weekend."

For some strange reason, Thomas felt something weird inside of him. He couldn't believe it, but he actually felt sorry for Vic.

"Why? How?"

"Every single person at school knows about that page, man," Carlos said. "Even the teachers."

"Oh, boy."

Carlos let out a low, laid-back laugh and then shook his head. "I bet he's fu-ri-ous."

"I better watch out."

"We got your back. No worries."

Carlos walked away in his casual strut as Thomas stuffed the bags in his hands into his locker.

They might have my back but they're not always going to be around to protect it.

He suddenly wondered if he had just made things worse.

Like a Circus in There

Kevin was heading over to the Salvation Army on Wednesday morning to bring the gifts that were already late when he got the call about Jenny. Not *from* Jenny but *about* her.

Lately, every time the phone rang, he got a little nervous. He mentioned it one evening to Jenny and she just laughed at him, calling him paranoid. But that was exactly what he was: paranoid. Worried that every call or knock on the office door or sudden groan from Jenny meant LABOR AND DELIVERY AND BABIES. He wanted just a little more time. Just a little more time to find Wonka's Golden Ticket, to discover a miracle under the Christmas tree, to wake up and be able to tell all his employees that they were doing just fine, thank you very much, let's toast to the new year.

But the call on the way to the Salvation Army changed everything.

"Kevin—we're at the hospital." It was Jenny's mom, who came out a couple times a week to help her out.

Here we go; it's game time.

"What happened—is Jen okay? Mom?" It was amazing that he could speak without being able to breathe.

"She's fine. She just fainted this morning."

"Fainted? Did she—is the baby okay?—are the babies okay?"

"Yes, they're fine. Everybody's fine. She's just a little dehydrated and tired."

A car honked behind him, and he realized that the light had turned green. He rolled down his window, ready to tell the guy behind him to take a hike.

What are you doing, Kev?

Instead he started down the road, then realized he was going in the opposite direction from the hospital. He could feel his heart beating, and he was consciously trying not to speed. He turned on the radio and cranked a loud rock song to try and get composed.

It's not gonna go loud enough to drown out the worries, Kev.

He stared down the road and knew that he had really truly no idea where it went. All he could do was stay in his lane and drive the speed limit and maybe he'd get there in one piece without an accident or a ticket or a breakdown.

*

The babies and mommy were fine. Kevin ended up spending the next hour with Jenny at the hospital. His mother-in-law went back home, where Grandpa was watching Gregory.

On their way out, Kevin held Jenny's hand and said nothing. He was finally able to compose himself and stop worrying.

In the car, before starting it, Jenny began to cry.

"Hey—sweetie—what's wrong?"

He held her for a while as she gently wept. "I'm fine, really," she said several times.

It was just her nerves and her fears and her hormones, Jenny said.

"You just got frightened," Kevin said as he held her in his arms in the hospital parking lot. "It's okay. Everything's okay."

"I just—I don't know what'd I do—Kev—"

"I know."

She didn't need to say any more. He knew the rest.

He glanced out a windshield that desperately needed cleaning. Then he closed his eyes for a moment, Jenny still in his arms.

"You know, every day I wake up and go to sleep thinking about our family and our future," he said. "It's so different from when we first got married. You know? I've always worried and always been anxious, I guess. But when Gregory came along, I realized that I had to worry about both of you. About taking care of this family. But that seemed doable. But sometimes—I don't know."

Jenny shifted and moved in her seat so she could look at him. She wiped her eyes with a tissue she'd pulled out of her purse. "What don't you know?"

"The thought of taking care of three. I mean—*three* kids."

She nodded. She got it.

"I know they say God doesn't give you more than you can handle, but I'm not so sure, Jen. I really sometimes don't know. I just—I know you think I worry too much."

"You do," she said.

"It's almost like I feel—I know this is weird—that it's my responsibility to worry."

"Who told you that?"

He shrugged. "I don't know. It's just—everything my parents went through when I was little—when Dad was out of a job and they struggled. I've felt like I've been doing everything I can to provide for us. I feel like I've gotten nowhere."

Jenny reached over and held his hand. Her eyes were red but still comforting and beautiful. "Nobody's ever ready. Especially for twins."

"Yeah. But if you could see inside my head." He laughed as he shook it. "It's like a circus in there."

"Is that supposed to be some big revelation?" Jenny asked with a smile.

"What?"

"I've known that since the day we started dating."

"Oh, really?" Kevin couldn't help smiling now.

"That's part of what I like about you."

"Shut up," Kevin said.

"Okay, only a little part. But it's true. That's just you."

He sighed, looking out the windshield and holding her hand.

"Let's not come back here for a while, okay?" he asked her.

"I'll try," Jenny said. "But it might not be up to me."

"Yeah. I'm afraid of that."

37

Lost Cause

It was Thursday morning. At seven-thirty Lynn had driven to stand outside the warehouse in line with others to get her presents. To get the kids their gifts. She'd been scheduled to show up at ten this morning, but she was supposed to be at an interview around then and was hoping they'd allow her to come in early.

Unfortunately, Lynn discovered that she had to wait until everybody who had the eight and the nine A.M. slots were taken care of. And it turned out, *a lot* of people were coming to receive gifts.

It was amazing how well organized everything was. The doors to the back of the hardware store opened up promptly at eight. There were several men and women from the Salvation Army inside the building, which had at one time been a warehouse that sold lumber attached to a hardware store in the front. One woman checked IDs while another verified names on a list. They would call out a number once the recipient was identified, then another person would ask what kind of gift wrap the recipient would like. Finally a couple of elderly men handed out what appeared to be small New Testaments to anybody who wanted them.

Except for the two Bible distributors and a few people in the back retrieving the gifts, all the men and women working for the Salvation Army were dressed in uniforms. The women had long skirts, the men pants, all of them wearing dress coats and ties.

After the third time of Lynn's asking if she could go earlier, the woman checking IDs told her it was fine. Lynn gave them her name and information and then said she was picking up for Thomas and Sara. They called out the numbers and several people walked to the back of the warehouse and began searching through red bags. That was the first time Lynn saw it. The bags.

There must be hundreds of them. Maybe even over a thousand.

They were red garbage bags full of presents. The people quickly brought her one bag that held the presents for Sara. But then she waited. And waited. And kept waiting.

And with each passing moment, she began to feel dread.

Please let them have his gifts, Lord. Please.

They had already received a huge—*huge*—answer to prayer with the money that she'd received from Daryl. She hadn't told the kids yet about seeing him but she wanted to. She not only wanted to, she intended to. The money had been a blessing but it hadn't gone very far. It had covered this month's rent.

But then there's January's rent. And February's rent. And so on and so on.

"Ma'am, I'm sorry, but you only have one bag."

Lynn looked around. She couldn't believe it. A room full of

hundreds of bags and they only had one for her? "There's got to be a mistake."

"I'm sorry. We've checked several times."

No, no.

"So who is this for?"

"Thomas Brandt. Can you check again?"

She was getting stares from the people behind her but Lynn didn't care.

"Ma'am, if you call our office tomorrow, we can try to see what happened to it."

Lynn stood there, not about to budge an inch, not about to worry about the long line of people behind her. She was here to pick up her children's presents, the ones she'd registered for with the good old Salvation Army, the ones that were supposed to be picked up a week before Christmas.

Thomas was right. He'd said that they probably wouldn't end up having any gifts for him.

"If I don't get them today, will I get them by Christmas?"

They might tell her that they would get the presents, but with her luck, *if* they ever showed up it'd probably be around Easter time.

The woman in the uniform gave Lynn an apologetic smile. But they had already checked the warehouse twice. To find a missing bag of presents would be almost impossible.

"Sometimes a name isn't chosen. But because of so many people's generosity, we have gifts for our Forgotten Angels."

Lynn felt insulted and humiliated and angry.

Sorry, Thomas, your presents didn't arrive. You're now an hon-

orary Forgotten Angel. Would you like your T-shirt that confirms this?

"If you come by tomorrow, we can make sure that you get some presents for your other child," the woman said in a patient tone.

"Some presents?" Lynn felt enraged. "I don't want some presents. I want the ones he asked for. That's how it works, right? I mean—that's how it's supposed to work! Isn't it?"

She could see the faces staring back at her, people behind her annoyed that she was causing a commotion and a delay, the faces of the twenty-something workers staring at her with that irritating look of compassion.

They're gifts, Lynn. You didn't earn them. You didn't pay for them.

But they didn't know what it took for her to simply sign up for this program. When she told Thomas and Sara about the program, it broke her heart.

A parent should be able to buy her children presents for Christmas.

Lynn wanted to keep fighting but she couldn't. She knew it was a lost cause.

"I'm sorry," the woman said to her.

"Yeah, I am too."

She sighed and lifted the red plastic bag full of presents for Sara. *God, why? Why Thomas? Why now?*

She left the warehouse and felt the bitter cold outside. Her hands felt as numb as her heart.

She didn't know what to do or where to go. All of Daryl's

money had gone to bills. She couldn't afford to buy Thomas much of anything.

As she sat in her car, she realized she was thirty minutes late for the job interview.

Lynn let out a scream of anger and frustration.

I hate this life of want. I hate it.

She started the Maxima. And naturally, it didn't start.

Lynn wanted to scream again but just waited in the cold quiet.

The car started after three tries.

As she pulled out of the parking lot, she felt too weary and dried up to shed a tear.

A Hero

Thanks to Vic, most of the students suddenly knew Thomas. Not only knew him, but wanted to make sure he knew that they knew. It wasn't just the kids bringing gifts to school for a noble cause, launched thanks to a Facebook page. But it was him walking down the hallway, getting looks of recognition and even an occasional "Hey Thomas" from people he didn't know.

Meanwhile, somewhere around Greer was a kid named Vic West who was probably devising another way to get back at Thomas.

Kids have guns around here, and every now and then some kid does something stupid.

Thomas knew he had to be careful.

But it was Friday, the last day before school got out. When the principal asked to see him right before lunch, Thomas thought that he might be in trouble. Instead, he discovered that Mr. Thornton had some surprising news for him.

"There's a camera crew from WYFF Channel 4 News to see you."

Mr. Thornton's thick eyebrows wiggled in a funny way that almost made Thomas laugh. He had more hair on his eyebrows than he had on his head.

"They want to talk to you about your Salvation Army project."

Thomas thought for a moment, surprised that the principal knew about it.

He gave it a name. The "Salvation Army Project."

Mr. Thornton guided Thomas to the front of the school, where for the next half hour he felt like he was a celebrity as the reporter asked him questions. It was around lunchtime, so a lot of students were looking at him. But for the first time in—well, maybe the first time *ever*—Thomas didn't mind the students looking. Maybe they knew that he was wearing the same ugly jeans and a two-dollar sweatshirt he'd gotten from the thrift store, but he didn't really care about that. Because they were probably also thinking how cool it was that he'd come up with an idea to do something good from something so bad.

"Where did the idea come from?" the pretty news lady named Jill asked.

"I don't know," he told her initially. Thankfully he wasn't being filmed yet. That's probably why she was asking him questions beforehand. So he could come up with decent answers.

But I really don't know why I did it.

"I guess I thought it'd be fun to see if some kids in the school would want to donate items to the needy," Thomas said.

The woman from the NBC news channel kept bringing up the terms *bullying* and *Facebook bullying*. But Thomas didn't want to go there. He didn't want to talk about Vic or about being a victim of bullying.

I'd rather not have Vic watch this and think of ten more reasons to drive over me with his pickup truck.

"I'm not really on Facebook much anyway," he said. "It was just a prank or something that someone did. Probably just for fun."

When they finally started taping, Jill asked him similar questions. Near the end, she asked him a question that hadn't come up before.

"But how do you feel now that this joke at your expense turned into an amazing act of generosity by Greer High School?"

Thomas shrugged and smiled. "I just know that—there's a lot of people out there that could use the stuff. I never thought that it'd turn out like this."

"So why did you choose the Salvation Army to bring the gifts to?" Jill asked.

"'Cause they really help people. I just figured—they do so much around Christmastime. Why not try to help out too?"

As Jill spoke into the camera next to Thomas, saying words like *brave* and *creative,* Thomas could feel his face blushing. There was a crowd around him and he suddenly wanted to get this over with and go back to normal life.

After the interview was over and he said good-bye to the reporter, he could see Cass standing near the entrance to the school.

"Hey," he said.

"You're a hero," Cass said.

"Not really. Just someone with an idea that actually worked."

"Very few people do things that actually work, Thomas. Not a lot of people know how to make a difference. That's what I think is so cool about all of this."

For a second Thomas thought about what she said.

To make a difference.

Then it dawned on him. His prayer. His prayer when he quoted Pastor Grady's words to make a difference, to try to help change a little something in this world.

"Here—this is for you," Cass said, handing him a sheet.

"What is it?"

"It's directions to my house."

The look on his face must've been stunned, because Cass laughed and quickly said, "It's for my New Year's Eve party."

"Oh, really?"

"Carlos has probably told you about it."

"Yeah, I think so," Thomas said.

But he couldn't act like it was no big deal. Of course he knew about it. Of course he was hoping she'd say something to him about it.

"Well, Mr. Change-the-World-Through-Facebook. If you actually ever checked your page, you'd realize that I sent you an invitation a week ago."

"Sorry."

Cass laughed and swept her blond locks out of her eyes. "It's a big party with a lot of people coming. Should be really fun. And—get this. I was inspired by you. I'm asking—no, I'm *making* people bring one item to donate to the Samaritan House afterward."

"That's great."

"I'm just copying you. But that's okay. Here are the directions in case you don't check out your Facebook page." She pointed at the paper Thomas still held in his hand. "I probably won't see you until then, right?"

For a moment Cass looked at him as if she was waiting on something. Thomas held up the sheet and thanked her for the directions, saying it sounded like fun.

Only later on, when he was sitting in class, did it dawn on him that her question hadn't been a simple comment.

That was a total setup. That was my chance.

"I probably won't see you until then, right?"

That was the moment he should have said, "Not necessarily." When he should have said, "I could see you tonight." When he should have said half a dozen other things instead of a lame "thanks."

He was completely and totally clueless when it came to girls.

The day's not over. Not yet, Thomas. There's still time.

Silent Night

The last day of work before the new year had turned out to be the last day of work for everyone at Precision.

Kevin had tried to figure out how to prevent this Friday from coming, but it was inevitable. He had talked to everyone individually at the company, so when he told them the news in the group meeting, it hadn't been a total surprise. There had been hugs and tears and a lot of sadness. Not just for people losing their jobs but also for Kevin, for the company he was losing, and for the people he was having to let go.

The day was surreal and exhausting.

Christmas was a week away and he felt defeated. He was the face of contemporary America, of a dream broken, of a journey at a dead end. Like so many others he'd seen on the news and read about online, Kevin was soon going to be out of a job.

He left the building after everybody was gone. He still had a little time left to work there and clean out the desks before the landlord asked for his keys. All he wanted to do was get home and try to put this day and this stormy year behind him.

*

Later that night, it turned out that the storm had followed him home.

The thunder came shortly after they put Gregory to bed. Kevin had just found a lone chocolate chip cookie that Jenny was willing to part with when Gregory howled. The terrified screams of their son sent Kevin running up the stairs to console him.

For some reason, the sound didn't merely scare Gregory. It petrified him.

"Stay with me, Daddy. Don't leave me."

The chocolate-chip cookie would have to wait.

"I won't," he told Gregory.

Gregory nestled in next to him as Kevin lay down beside him on the bed. The thunder boomed and the lightning streaked and the rain pelted the house.

"Daddy?" the little innocent voice said.

"I'm right here."

"I'm scared."

"It's okay. There's nothing to be worried about."

As his son's hands touched his arm and Gregory's face nuzzled against his shoulder, Kevin rested in the bed, looking up at the ceiling.

It was peaceful there. He wasn't online checking his e-mails, his phone messages, his Facebook or Twitter accounts, or worrying about any of that nonsense. He wasn't LinkedIn and that was fine.

He was lying next to his son assuring him that everything was going to be okay.

And it is going to be okay.

Sure. The lightning could strike down a tree that could crash into their house and this room. But that wasn't very likely. Instead, the threatening sounds and sights were really not threatening at all.

Gregory felt safe as long as Daddy was nearby.

The more Kevin thought of this, the more humbled he was.

He found tears streaming down the sides of his face.

Why can't I have the faith of a child, a faith so secure in his father?

He had a long way to go.

A long way.

In that bed next to his son, Kevin prayed that Gregory's two little brothers would be okay.

He really wanted to believe that God heard those prayers.

Kevin thought of a lyric from "Silent Night" that had been playing on the radio as he drove home: "Glories stream from heaven afar."

He wanted to believe that those streaming glories could reach Greenville, South Carolina, too.

The Storm

The rain pelted the thin tin roof of their trailer and leaked somewhere inside this tiny mouth of a bedroom. Thomas could hear the drops falling but couldn't turn on the light to find it since the power was out. He'd left his mother and sister in the living room talking by candlelight. He'd said he wanted to go to bed, but he really wasn't *physically* tired.

He was tired of being unable to do anything.

I might be some hero at the high school but here I'm still just the teen who can't provide for his mom and his sister.

Someone else should've been there.

Someone strong and faithful.

Someone they could look to for strength and faith.

Instead, his father was long gone.

In his room, Thomas realized there was a time in his life when he looked up to his father. It was before the drinking made him emotionally frozen like a statue and as undependable as the roof above him. Dad wasn't always like that. When he was younger, his father used to do things. A lot of things, in fact, like repairing stuff that needed fixing and cracking the occasional joke.

When Mom told them that she'd seen him again recently, it made Thomas hopeful that the man he remembered tiny glimpses of might still exist. Maybe he had changed again, this time for the good. Thomas wanted to know. He also wanted his father to know how they were doing.

I want to see him again. Before Christmas.

Mom still hadn't found a job, and he was still waiting to find one too.

Something tells me Mom didn't tell Dad the whole story about how we were doing.

The rain didn't soothe him. It seemed to bombard him with questions. About tomorrow and the next day and the next.

Trying to find a job, getting Mr. Sinclair to fix the roof . . .

Dad needs to know how we're doing. Maybe he can help us out. Maybe he'll finally get it that we can't do this on our own.

Kids not only deserved two parents but they needed them helping and supporting all along the way.

Mom couldn't do it all by herself. Thomas couldn't do enough to help out.

Just go see Dad and let him know.

It was there in the sanctuary of his cold room that Thomas made the decision. Just like he decided to combat something bad with something good.

He couldn't tell Mom, of course. But maybe then Dad would finally know how they were doing and what he'd done to them and maybe somehow things could get better. Maybe Dad would say he missed them and that he was sorry.

This'll be my Christmas present to Mom, he thought as the droplets of rain continued to fall in his room. *Maybe this will give her some kind of hope.*

And maybe, just maybe, one parent could end up turning back into two.

It was a Christmas miracle he could hope for.

The Man Inside

Do the dumb things our parents do mean we're doomed to fail just like them?

Thomas didn't know the answer.

They make choices just like everybody else.

He sat in the woods across the street from where they had lived and had been staring at it for a couple of hours now. It was the middle of the day.

He'd managed to get this far with the help of one of Carlos's friends at school and a truck driver. Mom would kill him if she knew he'd managed to make it all the way back to their home in Georgia. But for now she thought he was spending the day at Carlos's house. She thought he was doing something good, building friendships and starting to fit in.

She still doesn't know about the Facebook page. Sometime soon I'll tell her.

Thomas couldn't help being a little excited. He wanted to see with his own eyes. He didn't know what exactly, but he studied the house anyway. The truck was outside. He had not seen the front door open at all.

Over the past year since leaving, Thomas had never questioned his mother on why they'd left. They all knew. The biggest question Thomas had was whether or not their leaving had changed Dad.

After Mom told them about the money that Dad had given her, Thomas wanted to believe that his father had changed.

He wanted to get just a glimpse. Just a touch. Just something.

Some things in life just didn't add up and never would. Like why some really bad people seemed to have so much while people like his mother had nothing. Or why people like his father woke up and went to bed so angry at life. It always seemed to be guys too. He didn't get why some guys had to be so mean. Thomas had seen it all his life, and it was always males. And it always started with his father.

The troubles had always been over money. The bottle didn't seem to be necessary unless things weren't going well. When work didn't come, his father didn't shave. That black-gray stubble signaled trouble. It revealed a don't-give-a-hoot-about-anything attitude. It warned that it was time for the bottle, and the bottle meant the mean man would come back.

Dad didn't have big hands. But they sure hurt when he slapped Thomas around. His dad never hit him hard enough to land him in the hospital. But his father had hit him enough to leave marks—to leave bruises.

But the anger wasn't entirely predictable. It wasn't A plus B plus C equals D. It was more random, more ridiculous.

Like the time Thomas crashed his bike and came home late carrying it because the tire was shredded. His dad had flipped out and not spoken to him for a month. No hitting that time, just anger. It seemed so out of proportion to the incident. It was just a bicycle tire.

As Thomas thought of this, he saw someone pedaling down the street. Thomas ducked, then gasped. It was his father riding *his* bike. The very bike he'd had to leave behind.

What's he riding my bike for?

Dad got off and leaned the rusted-out bike against the side of the house, then walked up the steps to the porch. He suddenly turned around.

For a second Thomas thought he'd been seen.

Then his father went inside, banging the squeaky door behind him.

For a long time Thomas stared at the house and wondered about the man inside.

You've come all this way, Tommy boy. You gotta go inside.

He stayed hidden for a long time, crouched on some frozen leaves, watching. The wind made him cold and he knew he needed to go back to the truck stop not far away and see if he could catch a ride back to Greenville. He'd come back here to see if his father was still alive. And he was.

You came for more and you know it.

*

Thomas didn't know what he was going to find when he opened the door to the house. It was still their house and he still had every right to open the door. Maybe Dad was sitting in there reading the Bible and petting a dog named Sparky and listening to some old-time gospel hymns.

Instead, he found the very picture that he was hoping had been forever erased.

The bottle of whiskey was on the kitchen counter, two-thirds empty.

Dad sat in his armchair, the glass in his hand, the television on. He'd been in the house for an hour. That was how long it had taken Thomas to decide to go on inside.

Now he was wishing he had just gone back home.

When he stepped into the family room, the noise from the creaking floor made his father turn. He turned slowly, as if he couldn't care less if there were armed thieves ready to take everything and shoot him dead.

"What're you doing here?" Dad asked him.

The tone wasn't mean or nasty. But it was definitely drunk.

"I wanted to see you."

His father nodded, looking back at the television for a few minutes. A news show was on.

"Well, you've seen me. You can tell Mom all about it."

Thomas stood there, unsure what to do right now. So much had happened since he was standing here right before they left. So much had happened and yet he was back where he started. The same boy facing the same father in the same light.

"Mom's not doing so well."

"Really? What? She got sick or something?"

"She lost her job," Thomas said, standing up a little straighter, hoping to show that he wasn't afraid. "She hasn't found anything. And I'm trying to find a job, but it probably won't be much."

"Did she tell you kids that I just saw her? That I asked her when you'd be coming back?"

Thomas nodded but didn't tell his father anything more.

"Well, then. You can understand. That's what I get for trying to change. For trying to do something nice."

"You changed?"

His father shot him a glance that reminded him of the good ol' days. For a moment he wondered if he needed to get out of here. He was faster than his father, that Thomas knew for sure. Maybe he should haul out of here and take the bike and pedal all the way back home.

"Not a lot of good it did anyone," Dad said, looking away.

Something in the way he sat, a bit hunched over, looking thin and kinda sick and very sad, made Thomas feel something he'd never felt for his father.

Pity.

"I told her I'm sorry, and I'll tell you," Dad said, looking again at him. "I'm sorry. But I can't undo the past, Tommy."

"Why were you riding my bike?"

Dad shrugged, drained the last bit in his glass. "That's what happens when you get too many DUIs."

Thomas could feel the anger inside of him. He'd gone all this way to ask for his father's help. But his father was the same man they'd left. The past year had done nothing. Absolutely nothing.

"I gave your mother all the money I could," he told Thomas. "I'll get more to you when I can."

Thomas nodded.

That's all we'll need from you, and soon enough we won't even need that.

He didn't say anything but just glared at this old man. He could hardly call him a father.

"You want something?"

"Yeah," Thomas said. Then shook his head. "But I'm not gonna find it here. Not in this house."

He left without saying anything else.

Of all the grand and epic scenarios that had played out in his mind before coming here, he had never imagined that it would turn out like this. Another rerun of a show he was tired of watching night after night.

At least now I know.

Thomas thought of taking the bike that still was rightfully his, but he couldn't do that. His father could have it. But that was all he'd have.

Christmas Gift

Kevin sat looking at the screen, but he was having a hard time keeping his eyes open. He knew he needed to stop researching and take a break. Every lead only seemed to turn into another dead end. But he also knew that he didn't have time for breaks. He needed to make the most of every second of every day. Especially since his checking account was overdrawn and he wasn't expecting to get any checks anytime soon.

Santa might bring a lot of things, but he sure doesn't bring nice fat checks.

He still hadn't gotten Jenny's Christmas present, and he didn't know when he'd go out to find something. It wasn't the money for the gift. It just seemed ludicrous that in light of everything—with the twins coming and Jenny feeling sick and the company already gone under—that he would buy his wife something like gloves or jewelry or something *normal.* He wanted to give her something meaningful.

But lately all my energy and ideas have gone to Precision Design.

He wasn't always this way. He could still remember surprising her on her thirtieth birthday with a party full of friends and family. It had truly been a surprise, one that he had been proud to be able to pull off.

But the tendrils of life wrapped around him bit by bit as time passed. Now he felt like he was being suffocated as they squeezed and tried to snuff him out.

And that's before having twins. How's life gonna feel after having them?

With another doctor's appointment looming, and Christmas only a few days away, Kevin couldn't help feeling worried again.

He looked at a picture of Jenny and himself taken at Ray's wedding, sitting on his desk. The same Ray who was now getting a divorce.

The moments pass you by until you realize it's too late to get them back and say you're sorry.

He stood up and thought about going downstairs and then out for a walk. A coffee or a beer or something.

Then he looked back at his desk.

Don't leave these feelings deep inside of you. Do something with them. Let her know.

Kevin sat back down in his chair. He opened a new document and began to pour out his heart with two simple words:

Dear Jenny,

He thought for a moment, then he just started writing.

You deserve a lot more than this, than me. In the midst of the biggest event of both of our lives, I'm struggling with worry and the future. You encourage me when it should be the other way around. And it just dawned on me now, today, just how selfish and thoughtless I've been.

I'm sorry, Jen. I'm sorry for how little I've been there for you. I wake up knowing all the things I have to do but you never seem to make my to-do list. My priority list. My number one thing should be taking care of you, and I fail at that time and time again.

To be honest, I'm scared. Yes, I'm supposed to rely on God, but it just seems I have too much on my shoulders to share with anybody else. The business—the business. I sometimes wish that I could have had an easier path. I know that you signed up for so much better than this. You might say you signed up for me, but I haven't given you any of me lately.

I've spent a lot of time trying to figure out what to get you for Christmas. But it's stupid. I have a chance to give you gifts every day. Small, simple gifts. I'm sorry I haven't been there for you. Sometimes it's like I'm the one with the hormones and the twins inside of me. One can be called Worry. The other Work. Nice twins.

Kevin looked at the last line and thought about deleting it, then continued.

I sometimes fear that I'm going to wake up and find that I worked so hard for so long on what? For what? That I've missed all these gifts that have been waiting for me at my bedside. You and your grace. You and beauty.

You.

I can still do something about this. I can still change. I can still be the kind of person—the kind of husband—you need me to be.

Maybe. Hopefully.

This is my Christmas gift to you. Not the only one. But perhaps the most important. It's this promise.

I promise I'm going to try. Every day from here on out.

Okay?

I love you.

K

He saved the document but didn't print it out.

This time when he stood up, he left the office.

Kevin wasn't sure he'd give it to Jenny. He'd think about it.

Maybe he would later.

Maybe he wouldn't at all.

My Little One

That's the last time I'm going to rely on others. For anything.

Lynn barely glanced at the woman facing her in the old, scuffed-up mirror. She'd just finished brushing her teeth quietly as the kids still slept. She didn't need to examine the picture because she knew it too well. She felt the familiar bite again—the anger, the bitterness, the *why*s that followed her around.

She'd woken up realizing that today was December 23. After three more tries with the Salvation Army, Lynn had realized that Thomas wasn't getting his presents. Sometimes these things happened. They said that she could pick up the Forgotten Angel gifts but the whole situation just angered her. She didn't want consolation prizes. She wanted to give Thomas the gifts he'd asked for.

She had a couple hours this early morning to try to figure out something to get him. Then she had a couple of interviews that probably weren't going to amount to anything.

But really.

I mean, really, God? Really?

She didn't want or need anything, but for the love of all that was right—the kids deserved something. Anything.

Throw us a bone, will You?

Maybe this little trailer was too far off the map for God to hear her. Who knew how much longer they'd be able to live here too?

Fear had a way of suffocating her when she invited it in.

As she opened the squeaking door to leave the trailer, then opened another crunching door to her Nissan, Lynn realized the jacket covering her wasn't really warm at all. She shivered as she sat in the cracked seat and started the car.

The ignition switch wouldn't turn.

She tried a dozen times, then looked around the car as if a little gremlin might be sitting there with a devilish laugh.

"Are you serious?" she said out loud.

She kept trying but she had no luck. It wasn't the engine this time. She couldn't even turn the key an inch to try to start the engine.

She gripped the steering wheel and then pulled it as hard as she could.

"Come on!"

Hitting the seat next to her only filled the air with dust. She kept trying until the key broke off in the ignition.

That allowed her to let go of a couple of curses.

Then Lynn rested her forehead against the steering wheel and began to cry.

In the silence of that still morning, she wept.

Tears she barely recognized as her own kissed her cheeks and dropped into her lap. It was still dark and so eerily quiet that this old car felt like a coffin.

She didn't realize she was sobbing until the knock on the window startled her.

Outside in the shadows stood the tall shape of her son.

For a moment she was surprised at how tall he was.

You'll always be my little one, no matter how big you become.

She opened the car door.

"Mom?"

"It's okay."

"What's wrong?" His hair stuck up like it always did after Thomas woke up.

She sighed.

What isn't? Tell me that, Thomas.

"The car."

"Come on," he said, taking her hand.

"What?" Lynn just sat there in the car, trying to act like nothing was wrong.

"It's cold out here."

"I'm fine."

"Mom." He pulled her toward him.

"What?"

"Let's go inside."

She took her hand back and faced the windshield of the car. She was embarrassed that he had seen her like this.

"For what?" she asked.

"It's better than being out here doing nothing."

She glanced at him. He wore shorts and a T-shirt.

"Right?" Thomas asked.

She climbed out of the car and followed him back into the trailer.

*

After they'd been inside for a few minutes, Lynn decided to tell him.

"Your presents didn't come."

For a moment Thomas appeared unsure of what she was talking about.

"You mean the Christmas presents?"

She nodded as she held on to what was left of her car key, as if massaging it might help it regrow its other half.

"What happened?" Thomas asked as he got a glass of water from the sink.

"I don't know, and I didn't take any of the gifts they had for the Forgotten Angels . . ."

Thomas waited for more of a story, but nothing came.

"What about Sara's?"

"I picked up her presents the other day. They said that sometimes—every now and then—a registered angel isn't picked."

"So Sara got picked but I didn't?" Thomas asked. "Maybe Santa thinks I've been a bad boy this year. I knew I shouldn't a snuck behind Mr. Sinclair's house to steal his moonshine."

"It isn't funny," Lynn said. "And it has nothing to do with Santa."

He wouldn't be so mean.

"I'm sorry, Thomas. I know that this hasn't been the easiest year for you, not being able to play basketball and everything—"

"Mom?"

"What?"

"Are there a lot of these 'Forgotten Angels'?"

She shrugged. "I'm not sure. Maybe."

"So you think that if I had a stash of stuff, like clothes and shoes and games and toys and pretty much everything you can think of—you think that they could go to the Forgotten Angels?"

"I want you to get the gifts you asked for," she said.

As she looked at him, with his still-groggy eyes and bed head, she didn't know why a smile lit up his face.

"What?" she asked.

"Well, I was going to tell you eventually."

"About what?"

"Maybe if we get the car started, you can bring me to school."

Thomas kept smiling.

"Okay," she told him. "But first we have to get a set of pliers. Then find the spare key for the car."

The Only Thing

"Kevin."

The moment his wife uttered his name, he knew.

Jenny had climbed out of bed in her usual laborious manner that always made him feel empathetic. Her struggle to catch her breath, to stand up, to move slowly across the darkened bedroom floor. This time he'd heard her and then heard the flush moments later, followed by his name.

And the way she said his name didn't sound good.

"Yeah."

But he already knew.

It's time.

Of course, that was what he said every moment of every day. He was the child in the backseat asking, "Are we there yet?"

"I think something's wrong."

As he opened the bathroom door and his eyes adjusted to the light, Kevin knew. He didn't have to see the tears in Jenny's eyes. He'd heard them in her voice.

"I'm bleeding."

She was thirty-four weeks pregnant. She was scheduled

to go to the ob-gyn next week. At the doctor's last suggestion, Jenny had started taking steroid shots to help the babies' lung development in case . . .

In case of something like this.

This wasn't supposed to happen for another month.

But life, as Kevin had discovered more and more recently, had a way of doing things on its own.

It can't be now, not a day before Christmas Eve, not when there's still so much to do . . .

For a brief second time stood still.

A flickering assortment of moments shuffled through his mind—from the first day he really noticed Jenny to the first time they kissed to the moment she said yes to the moment she told him she was finally pregnant with Gregory.

"Okay," he said.

Adrenaline took over and they were ready.

Ready to start.

Ready to go.

Ready for whatever this looked like.

Stay calm for Jenny. Stay calm.

"Call my mom," the calmer of the two said.

"Okay," Kevin said.

"And get my bag."

"Okay."

He turned on the lights and gathered her bags, then called Jenny's mom and started to go to get Gregory out of bed when Jenny got his attention.

"You might want to put some clothes on."

Kevin looked down to see that he was only wearing boxers

with his shoes and coat. Old boxers that Gregory had picked out with Rudolph the Red-Nosed Reindeer on them.

"Yeah, okay," he said to Jenny.

He could feel the tremors going through him. With so many thoughts rumbling inside his head, Kevin couldn't seem to say a thing.

It was okay.

This wasn't a time to talk. It was a time to act.

*

There was no crazy delirious scene of Kevin getting in the car and forgetting Jenny. Everything was slow and steady so as not to cause her any more distress. She wasn't hurting but her worry wrapped itself all around her expression and motions. Jenny's mom was going to meet them at the hospital. Kevin had gotten Gregory up and put him in the car seat and thankfully a few minutes into the drive he was already going back to sleep.

Kevin held her hand tightly as they drove.

"It's going to be okay," he told her.

Jenny nodded but they both knew that it might not be okay. A lot of things in life weren't okay and this could turn out to be one of them.

The night seemed asleep with everybody resting up for the Christmas holiday. This was not the right time. It wasn't even Christmas Eve or Christmas day. It was the twenty-third.

He'd been distant from God for a long time. But now he didn't hesitate.

Lord, please let them be safe, please.

He knew that in the silence Jenny was praying too. Her

prayers probably held far more weight. She was the mother after all. She was the one who had more faith and who had gone before God more than just a few feeble times.

Please, God, please help Jenny and keep her strong.

Everything about the drive felt like slow motion. Everything. He was going a little above the speed limit. But the time seemed to sludge by and the street signs blurred while the thoughts and the memories and the fears inside of him blasted like hornets escaping a burst nest.

Suddenly all the thoughts and feelings and worries about work that had been plaguing him for the last few days and weeks and months seemed to melt away.

They meant absolutely nothing.

The only thing that meant anything was this woman next to him and the two lives inside of her.

God, please . . .

And God knew exactly what he was saying please for.

God knew.

The Weight of the World

He stands in a hospital gown looking like a lost child, pacing and helpless.

That's exactly what Kevin feels like. A child, lost and helpless.

All he can do is wait. Wait and pray.

The doctors are somewhere in an operating room getting Jenny ready for an emergency C-section. He looks like an extra from a television medical show who's waiting for his name to be called so he can stand in the scene and look busy but not quite do anything.

As he paces, Kevin understands something for the first time perhaps ever.

We are all children, lost, helpless, in need of a helping hand.

Like holding Gregory's hand.

His hand.

And as Kevin clasps his own hands, he thinks of God lending a helpful hand to him. It's such a cliché and such a commonplace image but it's true. It's true and it's real.

To be able to touch Jesus' robe.

Sometimes that was all it took to be healed and to have hope.

Sometimes it was just—one—simple touch.

"Give us two, God. Give us two."

That is what he prays.

He prays for Benjamin and Mark. They are real with defined personalities, Benjamin active and up all hours while Mark steadfast and quiet and strong. They have been alive for thirty-four weeks.

"Let there be more, God. Please."

He thinks of the wonderfully exquisite gift of life and then thinks of the Christmas cards and stamps and parades and Santas and songs all inundating the world right now.

It's not about asking; it's about receiving. It's not about the gifts but about the gift.

There is a small cross on the wall that he notices. Something small that someone of faith probably put there. He stares at it for a long time and shudders. He thinks of that poor mother kneeling by the manger. The terrified father surely out of his mind. And the weight of the world on their shoulders as creation waited, holding its breath, anticipating the utter glory of this beautiful creation.

Their son. His Son.

"I wouldn't give my son up—not in a million years—not in a second would I ever give one of mine up, Lord."

His heart races and he can't understand how God could do something like that. All he wants is to hold Jenny's hand and kiss her cheek and know she is okay. To see the sweet, angelic faces of his two sons and know they are okay.

Yet You allowed Yours to come to this rotten failing place in order to die.

Suddenly Christmas and the very notion of what the word *gift* truly means hits Kevin with full force.

The door opens and the nurse asks him to come with her.

And Kevin nods and follows her.

Please come down and help us out. Please, God.

And walking down that white, sterile hallway to the operating room where Jenny is ready for an emergency surgery, Kevin realizes something else.

He is not a designer or a businessman or an entrepreneur or an artist walking down this hallway.

He is just a father, praying and hoping that his sons will be okay.

That is all he is, and that is all that matters.

Receiving

It was in the early minutes of Christmas Eve when Kevin and Jenny got their answers.

He stood next to her, reassuring her, smiling at her, kissing her forehead. All he had eyes for was her round, angelic face beaming up at him. The rest of the sounds in the room went away. It was just the two of them, like on their wedding day after her father gave him her hand.

It's just the two of us from here on out.

But in a strange way, Kevin felt like they were surrounded by a whole host of faces watching them. Watching and waiting. Watching and helping. Not the doctors and nurses but a roomful of angels looking after them.

It was a nice thought. Perhaps an overly hopeful, delirious thought. But it filled him and gave him strength to smile.

The first baby's cry was hoarse and strangled. The doctor talked calmly to him. Kevin stood behind the blue sheet with Jenny, waiting to see what their Christmas presents looked like. Waiting to unwrap them and hold them.

Tears rounded his eyes and he smiled out of pure joy, waiting, looking down at Jenny, then looking back up to see the doctor's face.

He used to think the best part of Christmas was the waiting.

But, like many things in his life, Kevin decided he was wrong about that.

It wasn't about waiting.

The true joy came in receiving.

The Sign

Mom had brought them to a Christmas Eve service that had been simple and short. At the end everybody in the sanctuary held lit candles and sang "Silent Night." It had been a while since they'd gone to church, and even though Thomas was glad to be going, he couldn't help being distracted. The entire time he sat in the pew, he thought of his father, probably sitting in his usual place back at their house, drinking his night away and drowning whatever sorrows he could come up with. It made him angry that they were there and his father was somewhere else. It made him angry that all this time hadn't changed the man he still loved but no longer respected.

As they left to go back home, Thomas saw a lit-up sign alongside the road next to the church's parking lot. He hadn't spotted it when they first walked into the Baptist church. Underneath the name of the church and the time of the evening service, there was a quote:

IF ANYONE DESERVES TO CARRY A GRUDGE, IT'S CHRIST. BUT INSTEAD, HE CARRIED A CROSS.

He wondered if an angel had wandered down the road and put up the letters that seemed meant just for him. As they started to leave the parking lot, Thomas was glad it was dark outside.

That way Mom couldn't see the tears coming down his cheeks.

All His Heart and All His Soul

He could still hear her sleeping when he opened his eyes to darkness on Christmas morning.

The haggard breathing of a woman in pain, a woman on painkillers and almost knocked out. A woman resting thirty hours after her prized bout and Super Bowl and World Series all rolled into one.

Kevin put on some shoes and slipped out of the room. He felt an emptiness even though it was seven on a morning when he should be full. Families would be gathering around trees and opening presents but they had already done that.

They'd had a whole day to deal with the news that Christmas Eve brought.

He walked the familiar hallway hearing the silence.

It's going to be okay.

He could do this. He could.

Just one breath after another. One hour after another. One day at a time.

He felt half there, a spirit split in two.

It took only a few moments to get there.

He did the regular ritual, signing in and scrubbing, then stepping next to half-closed curtains.

Then he saw them.

Both of them in individual beds, both so tiny, both fast asleep, both alive and doing well.

Both.

Kevin didn't know who to go to first.

He chose the smaller one in the enclosed clear bed.

"Good morning, Benjamin."

The little boy, only three and a half pounds but long and content and thankfully *healthy,* seemed to hear his voice. He wiggled and moved slightly, then opened his eyes.

Then he did something quite unexpected in his day-old life.

Benjamin smiled.

Maybe it was just the motion of trying to move his lips, but Kevin didn't believe that. He saw a smile on the face of the tiny one who gave them a scare, the one he prayed over and bargained with God for, the one who was so eager to come out and meet them.

The one Jenny had asked him about as he stood next to her with the drape separating them from the babies.

"How does he look?" Jenny had asked.

Just like his twin brother before him, Benjamin had looked shriveled up, with the face of an old man, but he had also looked absolutely "Beautiful," Kevin had said.

The anxiousness had been there until they had brought both babies over briefly to introduce them to Mommy and Daddy. As the little lives cried, their heads touching as they hovered over Mommy, Kevin had known.

They're okay. Both babies are okay.

He'd been so worried and so lost and so weak and yet . . .

Yet here he stood hours later, a day later, looking at Benjamin, who had smiled with a smile that said, *No need to worry, Pop.*

That said, *What took you so long to come back around?*

It said everything in its innocent helplessness.

A tube came out of Benjamin's nose. The feeding tube. Another set was attached to his hand. A backdrop worthy of a *Star Trek* scene stood in the background.

But all Kevin knew was that Benjamin was okay, just like his brother Mark. All things considered, both babies were doing well and were healthy and in very good, capable hands.

Kevin walked back over to the other side of the room separated by a curtain where Mark was resting. They looked the same, though different. Mark was a little chunkier and seemed to enjoy sleeping for the moment. He was the one who had been head down inside of Jenny.

Looking at his son, Kevin once again thanked God for this gift, for these two gifts.

*

In the cafeteria, Kevin sat with caffeine in hand and wolfed down a bagel and some yogurt.

He was still riding the wave of adrenaline with little sleep.

For a moment, however, he sat still and looked out the window and watched the sunrise.

What a glorious and good day.

He took a sip of coffee and thought that this morning had started with two of the most glorious sunrises he'd ever seen.

It was strange, but life suddenly had absolute purpose. Everything had a whole new meaning, a different shade, an alternate weight, a higher cause.

Help me to be the father I want to be, that I need to be. Help me to be a good man and husband to my wife and those boys.

This was something he knew. He was going to love those boys with all his heart and all his soul. Sure, he would let them down, but when he did he was going to make it right because they were gifts and they were angels and they had a father who was going to do every single thing he could to be a good one.

With Mommy's help, of course.

Life for the moment was on pause. At rest. Jenny was recovering from the C-section in her hospital room. Gregory was at home with the grandparents. The babies were in the NICU under the good care of nurses like Jean the patient one and Julie the one with the English accent and Stef the tough but good-hearted one. In his state, he was lucky to remember their names and faces.

He let out a sigh of relief and thankfulness and joy.

Then, he uttered a prayer in the quiet of this morning and this empty cafeteria.

"Thank You, Father. Thank You for helping out. Thank You for lending me a hand through this, for guiding me across the busy street, for bearing my worries and my fears . . ."

Kevin stared at that glowing sun that was a reminder of so much on this day.

"Thank You for picking my name off a tree and giving me two amazing and precious gifts that I never deserved and will never be able to repay you for."

And just like that, Kevin remembered.

The presents for Thomas.

"Oh, no."

It was Christmas day, and the presents that he bought for the paper angel named Thomas were still in the trunk of his car, waiting to be delivered.

Waiting to be presented to a boy who was surely disappointed and wondering what had happened to them.

Where You're Going

Sara and Thomas had managed to get Mom a stockingful of gifts that they'd individually wrapped to make Christmas morning feel special. They were small things that both of them had bought at the dollar store and Target for a buck. But Mom didn't mind. She opened up each one as if it were fine jewelry. The tears in her eyes spoke her thankfulness.

Sara had opened her gifts and couldn't believe she received everything that she'd asked for. Thomas could tell that she felt bad about his not receiving his Angel Tree gifts, but it didn't matter. After all the giftgiving this year, including bringing all the donated presents down to the Salvation Army to give to their "Forgotten Angels," Christmas had already been beyond special. He'd always remember this year because of that. Because of that and because of the way those silly little presents made his mom cry.

As they sat in the trailer with the Christmas tree in the corner decorated with homemade ornaments and paper chains, the sound of Christmas music on the radio, Mom disappeared for a moment and then came back with something.

"I know you didn't get the presents you asked for," Mom told him, presenting him with the square gift wrapped in red and green. "But this is from your sister and me. Sara wanted to make sure you knew it was from her."

"Uh-oh," Thomas said.

"Open it," Sara said.

Holding the box, he already half guessed what was inside it. But he didn't want to really believe that. There was no way. It couldn't be.

When he saw the box, he knew it was indeed true.

He smiled and opened the top of the shoe box.

"They're not Nikes but they're new and look durable."

"And *I* helped pick them out," Sara said.

They were new basketball shoes.

It didn't matter what brand they were or exactly what pattern or style was on them. They were *new* basketball shoes.

"Mom," he said, wondering how she got the money to pay for them.

"You needed them. I just wish—"

But before she could finish that comment, Thomas got up and gave her a hug.

*

Later on that Christmas morning, in the quiet of his room as he wore his new basketball shoes, Thomas opened up the notebook and began to write.

It was a letter he needed to write.

He thought again about the church sign he'd seen after spending the entire service loathing his father.

I don't want to spend any more time hating that man.

In his mind, he tried to picture that man he'd seen riding his old bike. The man who was still in their old house. The man who was becoming old just like that place, just like his habits.

I can still believe and I can still hope to be surprised.

His room was quiet. Thomas felt cold as usual.

What could he say?

What words were there for the man who had hurt them?

Thomas looked at the sheet of paper. For a moment all he felt was despair. Everything seemed wrong—it was the wrong kind of paper, the wrong approach, the wrong everything.

He wasn't typically so unsure of himself.

But this was different.

In a sense, he was writing to himself, for himself, for his family.

I'm just writing a guy who was once fifteen too.

He was fifteen but knew the world was big and that roads were wide open.

It's not where you've been but where you're going.

And maybe, just maybe, Thomas could write to his father on this day, forgetting about the past and bringing them up to the present.

Hello, I'm Thomas, your son, your one and only son.

Thomas forced himself to write.

He wanted this to be as natural as if he were talking to his father in person.

He wrote the letter still believing that his Christmas presents might arrive, still hoping and believing that they would show up at the door.

Guys like Vic at school could belittle and laugh and ignore him. But they could never take away the very thing that he still considered his greatest strength.

His faith.

And this crazy notion of taking the bad and doing something good with it.

Thomas let out a deep breath and started to write the words to the man who surely didn't want to hear them.

After he was finished, he sat there for a moment, looking at the two words right above his name.

Merry Christmas.

So common and so casual.

Christmas doesn't have to come once a year. It can happen every day.

This faith came down to that very gift that spawned this holiday.

The point was that one gift was for the rest of the year, for the rest of ever after.

He folded the note and then left it on the tiny dresser in the corner of the room.

He could still send it out. Even after Christmas.

Gifts didn't have to always arrive in time for Christmas.

And Christmas didn't always have to arrive at the same time each year.

Home

The beauty of being a child was growing up full of dreams and aspirations. You always carried them around with you, these pocketfuls of potential.

Lynn knew this too well. But she also knew something else—the danger of being an adult. Somctimes you reached an age where you reached into your pocket and found nothing. Those dreams had been stored away in a shoe box and tucked in the corner of a crawl space somewhere. Many times, you didn't have the time or the energy or the desire to go find that shoe box and dust it off and look inside.

Adulthood sometimes—many times—meant the shoe box was never found again.

Lynn thought of this not in terms of her life but in terms of Thomas and Sara. If there was anything she wanted from here on out, regardless of what would happen today and tomorrow and the next, it would be for them not to lose their hopes and their dreams.

And for that not to happen, she had to be an example. She needed to learn how to dream again, and that started by gaining her footing again and swallowing her pride and taking it a day at a time.

It's Christmas day and Thomas and Sara and I deserve a nice, home-cooked meal.

So she told them to get into the car, and then she prayed that it would start. Thankfully, the Maxima wasn't finished just yet. She told them that they were going out for their Christmas dinner. For a few brief moments Thomas and Sara seemed mortified. Sara asked if they were heading over to Uncle Jesse's house. She told her no, that she wouldn't do that to them.

As she drove, Lynn thought about the reaction that Thomas had to the basketball shoes. In that moment he'd been her little boy again, not this tall, teenage boy living with her. Thomas had always had a gentle spirit, and even though he still carried it with him, she couldn't forget that he was a fifteen-year-old. His display of raw emotion told her that she'd overreacted about the missing presents. She'd been angry and vocal about that with God but He'd shown her who was boss and what really mattered. Thomas didn't care about the gifts from a list. He was simply glad to be there, with her and Sara.

God does that quite often in ways I don't really like.

It was shortly after noon and she had made her decision.

Pride was a hard thing to swallow sometimes.

So was thankfulness in the wake of a raging storm.

She didn't tell the kids where they were going. They were just going. It was an address downtown and it would surely be busy. There would be others like her, even more broken and bruised, waiting just like they would be for a warm meal. For the simple creature comforts of something that tasted good and filled the stomach and the soul.

Just a meal.

Nobody was too good to be standing in that line. Not her. Not Thomas or Sara. Not anyone.

They parked close and walked on the sidewalk as she locked arms with her two angels and knew that it would get better.

The sign that said it all with the words CHRISTMAS DINNER was the place they were going.

Seeing the smile on Thomas's face was the only present she wanted and asked for.

Entering the doorway, Lynn knew that this wasn't the end but the beginning of something that could be special. It was all how she looked at it. Just like Thomas taking something mean-spirited and creating something good out of it.

God is good even when the world out there can be cruel and mean.

The room was full of people. Laughter and conversation filled the air. There wasn't any shame being here, just the shame Lynn had held in feeling like this was beneath her. She smiled at her kids and then led them to one of the lines. The scent of turkey and gravy and stuffing and candied yams swirled around her.

Lynn imagined heaven smelled a lot like this.

Home.

Under the Tree

It was late afternoon on Monday, the day after Christmas. Sara was at a friend's house and Thomas was somewhere playing basketball. Lynn waited for both of them to come home. Especially Thomas.

Four things awaited his arrival. Four things she stood looking at as if they were magical illusions that might go away if touched.

The four presents were probably the most extravagantly wrapped gifts she had ever seen. And somehow, in some miraculous way, those four presents all had Thomas's name handwritten on their stickered tags.

The woman delivering them apologized and said she was doing a favor for the frantic man who was late in handing them in.

"He just had twin boys, so he's half out of his mind," the round-faced woman told her with a beaming smile. "I promised I'd come here so you got these presents before it was too late."

Now the presents sat in their trailer like a lantern on a dark and stormy night.

It didn't matter that they weren't under some glorious Christmas tree, just their little donated tree with the paper chains.

The presents seemed to dwarf the tree they sat under, as if the Star of Bethlehem was centered on the ground and pointing upward instead of vice versa. One was solid gold wrapping, another in the image and colors of a candy cane, and another a classic red and green.

The biggest box was a red, black, and white collage.

Something told Lynn that the red, black, and white weren't just random colors.

At least I hope they aren't. I really, really hope!

She could hardly wait for Thomas to come home and open them.

*

"Come on, open them already!"

Thomas shook his head in silence. It was close to eight and Thomas wasn't budging.

"You're not going to open them tonight?" Lynn asked.

"Nope."

He'd gotten home a little after seven, all sweaty and tired from playing ball all afternoon. Thomas had grabbed dinner at Carlos's house. When she told him to look under the tree, he seemed confused.

But after taking a shower, Thomas had decided to leave the presents there until the morning.

"Why don't you want to open them now?" Sara asked.

She seemed more excited for Thomas to open them than he did.

"Because I just—'cause I have my reasons."

"You can open them whenever you like."

He nodded, then studied them. "I like having them under the tree. Just sitting there waiting to be opened."

Lynn nodded, still not quite understanding why he waited. She still couldn't believe that after everything, the gifts had arrived.

I wish I could thank the man who bought them. Perhaps thank his wife and give them a little something for their two new additions.

"You didn't think they'd come, did you?" she asked Thomas, messing up his hair.

"I was planning on them coming, to be honest," he said.

"Looks like we get to celebrate Christmas morning twice this year," Lynn told them.

"Yep," Thomas said with a mischievous look on his face.

Paper Angels

In the wildness of the past few days, it was easy for Kevin to overlook the gift God had given him several years ago.

Why is it so easy to blame God for unanswered prayers and so easy to forget the ones He answers?

Kevin parked the car and glanced at his son in the backseat.

"You doing okay?" he asked.

"Uh-huh."

They had just been jamming to a little Brooks & Dunn as he drove Gregory to his aunt Becky's house. He thought of how excited Gregory had been to meet the twins. Now it was early morning, and though Kevin's life had seemed to erupt, his firstborn was doing remarkably well.

He climbed out of the car and then unbuckled his brute of a son. Gregory walked to the familiar front door and rang the door bell several times. But before the door opened, Kevin took his son's hand.

"You know something?"

His cute, optimistic face looked up at Kevin. "What?"

"I love you."

"I love you too, Daddy."

It was the sort of comment that was true and unabashed.

Gregory smiled and gave him a hug.

We prayed long and hard for you and God answered those prayers.

When Kevin's sister came to the door, he spent a few minutes updating her on Jenny and the twins. Gregory was already inside, ready to play with his favorite aunt.

"Thanks for watching him."

"Please," Becky said. "Just let me know when I can see those cute little babies again."

"Will do."

Climbing in the car, the sun shining, Kevin was thankful. Overwhelmed, exhausted, but thankful.

*

Thomas woke up Sara with the first present. He stood on the edge of her bed and then nudged it. It took a few nudges to get her to open her eyes.

"What?"

"I have something for you."

Sara's Christmas gifts were on the floor next to her bed. There was an American Girl board game, a few outfits that all kinda went with one another—not that Thomas really could tell for sure—a set of teen paperbacks with white covers and spooky-looking images on them. Somewhere in the room was the perfume that he'd teased her about.

Sara turned over and tried to go back to sleep.

"You might like this," he said.

"Christmas was yesterday."

He put the card next to her on the thin sheet.

His sister turned again and peeked out. Seeing the red card, she was curious.

"What is that?"

"You have to open it."

"Why now?"

"Because I have important things to do," Thomas said.

"Like what?"

"You want me to take this back?"

She shifted and pulled herself up. A hornet's nest of hair needed to be pulled away from her face.

"That's one of your presents."

"Open it," he said, enjoying this but also annoyed at how irritating she could be.

Sara took a minute to decide like all the girls he'd ever known. Then she took the card and opened it.

For a minute she just read it, then looked at him, then read it over, then looked at him again.

The message was short and sweet.

I hope this makes you a little more happy. Even if it's a little late.

You deserve it.

Your big brother

Sara paused for a moment, then opened the present.

It was a brand-new iPod.

"Thomas! Did you ask for this?"

"Does it matter?"

"Did you really get this from your Angel Tree? From the gifts that came yesterday?"

"You want it or not?"

She shook her head in disbelief, her eyes wide, her face almost white with surprise.

"But you—"

"Look, if you're going to be the next Taylor Swift or American Idol, you gotta know a lot of songs."

Yes, Sara might be annoying at times. And yes, she might be younger than he and sometimes thoughtless and most definitely a *girl*. But he still loved her. And he just wanted—just hoped—just wanted to see . . .

"Thanks," Sara said.

And then it came.

Her smile.

The smile that he'd missed for a very long time. Much too long.

This was a selfish gift for himself.

To see Sara smile.

*

"I almost forgot this."

It was late and Jenny was actually starting to be able to stand on her own after the C-section from a few days ago. But now she was sitting in the hospital bed finishing up her dinner.

"What's this?" she asked.

"It's a letter I wrote and wanted to give to you before Christmas."

She took it but then he told her to hold off on reading it for now.

"Read it sometime when I'm not here. Otherwise I'll feel all stupid."

Anybody else would ask him why, but not Jenny. She just smiled into his eyes.

"Okay."

"How are you feeling?"

"A little better," she said. "The shower helped."

"You're doing great. You really are."

"Not the way I expected to spend Christmas."

"It's okay by me. Now that everyone's doing fine."

"Speak for yourself," Jenny said with a playful grin.

Kevin smiled. He looked at her and knew she was stronger than he was and always would be.

*

Thomas knocked on the partially closed bedroom door. He heard his mother say "Yeah?" and he walked in. She'd changed into her sweatpants and sweatshirt after a day of interviews that didn't go particularly well.

"You still up?" Mom asked him.

"I wanted to make sure Sara didn't bother us."

"What's up?"

"I wanted to give you something."

"Thomas—"

"Here."

He handed her the box.

"No," Mom said.

"What?"

"If that's what I think it is, then no. Absolutely not."

"Mom."

"Sara told me what you did. You gave her one of your Christmas gifts?"

"Just open it."

She stood there, holding the box, shaking her head.

"Thomas—I don't know—"

"You're not going to get all emotional, are you?"

She shook her head, laughed, and then wiped at the tears in her eyes.

"I just don't get you," she said.

"What?"

"I can't . . . I mean, where'd you get that? Where?"

He looked at her, confused, then turned his gaze to the bed squished into the corner of the small room, his gift resting on top of it. Thomas felt embarrassed and nervous, like he'd done something wrong.

"What?" he asked.

"Where'd you get that heart of yours? I just—it sure wasn't from your father. Or me."

"Just open it."

She shook her head and then lifted the card attached to the present.

And that was when the tears really flowed.

"Thomas," she said after reading it.

"Keep going."

After she opened the present to find the digital camera, Mom placed both the card and camera onto the bed and gave him a hug.

"It's true," he said.

Mom hugged him harder than she'd ever hugged him before. She held on to him and began to sob. He wasn't sure if she was happy or sad.

"I didn't mean to upset you."

"I'm not sad, Thomas. I'm not sad. I'm just awestruck."

She let go of him eventually and picked up the card again.

"Was this your intent all along? When you asked for all of these things?"

"No. Not at first. But I just—it seemed like a good thing to do."

She read the card again as if she hadn't read it quite right the first time.

Just like Sara's card, this one was short and sweet.

To Mom:
Merry Christmas to the prettiest girl
I've ever known.
Love,
Thomas

*

It was late and Kevin was returning from making sure Gregory was tucked in at Aunt Becky's house. She would be watching him again while Kevin stayed at the hospital one final night with Jenny. He parked in the familiar parking lot at the hospital. Then he sighed as the cold wind blew against him. For a moment, before opening his car door, he thought about the gifts he finally delivered to the Salvation Army yesterday, then he looked up to the dark heavens.

Sometimes You make us wait too, don't You?

He thought of the gifts going to some kid he didn't know, to some young kid who probably thought he'd been blown off.

Then he thought that in some ways, he probably wasn't much different from that kid.

I don't have faith, Lord. I don't trust You. I'm impatient. And I'm so full of doubt.

He climbed out of the car and dug his hands into his pockets. Kevin took a quick glance around the empty parking lot.

Then it dawned on him.

He was a paper angel just like Thomas. God picked out his name a long time ago and knew exactly what was on his list—gifts that He handed out at just the right time, just when he needed them.

That didn't mean everything on the list was going to show up at his door. But God knew what his list looked like.

God also held the paper angel in His hand.

In His hand.

He felt a shiver that had nothing to do with the cold. He prayed for the boy he didn't know and the family the boy belonged to. Then he headed toward the hospital, back to three-fourths of his family, a family whose unknown names he'd once written on a list and hung on a tree and prayed that he would one day have the great fortune to meet.

Kevin couldn't wait to see those two little new faces again.

To see their random smiles.

In this world, a smile was a beautiful thing. A gift.

The Shoes

It's twenty minutes till midnight, and Thomas still has every intention of hugging and kissing the host of the party. But first he has Vic to deal with. He has arrived at the New Year's party smelling like cheap beer and clearly having one thing in mind: payback. Payback for getting kicked out and made a fool of by Thomas.

Thomas laughed at the thought. Some stories might end that way, but not this one.

It wasn't nighttime yet. There was still the party at Cass's to go to. As much as he'd like to think that he'd be even near the host of the party, he was just glad to be going somewhere. To have friends to be with.

But the party was hours away. He still had some unfinished business to deal with.

*

The squeaks and grunts in the gym sounded like heaven to him. Thomas liked to think that there would be lots of ball played up in heaven. Except there would be no hard feelings after the game was over. There'd be no anger and jealousy and silliness.

He sat and waited for the game to be over. It was just five-on-five using half the court while another game happened on the other half. A couple of times Thomas was told to put on the shoes he was holding and join the game. Thomas just smiled. Once it was over, he zeroed in on the guy glancing at him with malicious eyes. He followed him to the water fountain, then as Vic headed back to the seats where their bags were, he said, "Hey Vic."

The guy ignored him, so Thomas said his name louder.

This time, Vic stopped and turned. The face and body language seemed to say that it was time. It was time for someone to get hurt.

"I got something for you," Thomas said.

Then he walked over and handed Vic the Nikes he'd been carrying. Vic didn't take them, so Thomas shoved them into his chest.

"These are yours."

Vic glanced at them. Surely he knew that they were the latest and greatest basketball shoe Nike made. Even if he couldn't afford them, it didn't mean he wouldn't have looked in the window or seen the ads on television.

"Is this one of those presents someone put in your locker?"

Thomas had rehearsed this several times, but he could taste the fear racing through him.

"Look—this is the way I see it," he said. "If we're ever going to be teammates, then one of us has to make a peace offering. And I figure it might as well be me."

There was a genuine look of confusion on Vic's face.

"Take them. I was hoping—I was planning to get them to you before Christmas. But a few days later is okay, right?"

"You're seriously giving these to me?"

"Yes."

"What? Are they stolen?"

Thomas laughed. "No. The receipt is there in case you don't wear elevens."

Vic looked around, then stared at the shoes. "What's the catch?"

"No catch. Except that maybe you don't have to act like you want to pound my face every time you see me."

"So you're paying me off?"

"No. That's just—well, you can use them, right?"

Vic glanced down at his shoes and seemed to get it.

"I remember your shoes not looking too hot either."

Thomas wasn't wearing his basketball shoes, neither the old ones nor the new.

"Someone gave me some new ones."

"I'm not some charity case," Vic said.

"Charity?" Thomas asked, laughing. "I want to make sure you can keep up with me."

Then Thomas nodded and left.

Part of him wondered whether Vic was going to throw the shoes at his back or perhaps toss them into a bonfire.

Who knew if this would change anything? But Thomas wanted to believe that it could and would.

A Piece

The gift waited for him like a child on the porch. He could see it as he climbed off the bike and walked slowly toward it. He paused for a second, then continued. The afternoon's glare caused him to squint. He wiped his hands on dirty jeans as he took the familiar steps and then stood before the package.

Sometimes a man reached a point in life where there were no surprises.

If there was such a place, it was right here. It was a dusty dead end, another drained beer can, an empty pack of smokes, a barren shell that echoed all the *might-haves* and *could-have-beens.*

He opened the gift carefully. It'd been some time since he'd gotten a gift. It had his name on it but it still felt like some joke, like the boys back at the plant were pulling his leg, like the guys at Larry's were playing a trick. His dirty fingers picked and pulled off the gift wrap. It took a good few minutes to finally open it up and see what was inside.

It was a box. Unmarked and taped shut.

On the box was a note.

He read it and the words colored his eyes and his mind like blood in water. For a minute he couldn't do anything. He couldn't breathe or think or read or act or do anything. All he could do was shut his eyes and feel the pain in his soul.

It wasn't right. It just wasn't right.

But he opened his eyes unsure whether there were tears in them or not. It'd been some time since he got all girlie and cried like this. But something inside was broken and something else was gushing out of those cracks.

His hands shook as he went to open the box. He wanted and needed a drink but more than that he wanted and needed to open this.

For a second the shaking seemed to consume his entire body. He let go of the box and tried to straighten his hands. For a moment he wondered if anybody was around. But nobody was here. Nobody came down here. Ever.

Nobody except young visitors who let themselves in only to get let down.

He pried open the top and then looked inside.

The colors were unmistakable.

The number was without question.

He touched it and could tell right away that this was real. This was no fake or knockoff.

This was the real deal.

Then the words from the note came to his mind and he knew.

The dots didn't connect because there were too many of them. But he at least understood the meaning behind the words.

The man picked up the letter again and reread it.

The words there were more valuable than this jersey with the bold number 23 on it.

Dad,

You taught me that Michael Jordan wasn't just some amazingly talented kid. He also worked really hard at the one thing he loved. That's what I am going to do. And you can do it too.

I'm not giving up on you, Dad. I'm not going to—I can't—keep a grudge either.

Maybe in time—and with a lot of hard work—we can be a family again.

God bless you, Dad.

I love you,
Thomas

Daryl Brandt hadn't realized till that moment that he was kneeling on the battered porch of his house.

This wasn't just a Chicago Bulls jersey in this box. It wasn't just an autographed Michael Jordan jersey.

This was a piece of his son and a piece of him. This was a part of their story. Minuscule but miraculous nevertheless.

He swallowed and looked up into the sky.

The hand that still shook wiped the tears off his cheek. He nodded toward the heavens. That was all he could do, but it was more than he'd done for years. For decades.

Daryl wondered if that story was finished. If the stories with all of them were done.

He could only hope they weren't.

Epilogue
The Following July

Unbelievably, there was silence in the house.

Kevin sat on the deck with Jenny. The twins were inside asleep, and Gregory was at McDonald's with Grandma.

Silence was as golden as the sky above them.

"So, are you ready?" Jenny asked.

He looked at his wife and smiled. "I'm not really sure."

"Why?"

Kevin sighed. "It's been seven months since I've taken a business trip."

"You've been a little busy."

"We both have."

"It's going to be great. *You're* going to do great."

Kevin nodded and looked at the trees that he had planted ten years ago. It was amazing that tiny little twigs they'd bought at Home Depot could be so massive and sprawling.

"I always thought that things would be different," he told Jenny. "That the aftermath would be more traumatic after shutting down Precision."

"When did you shut it down?"

Jenny often teased him because it was true—he hadn't really closed the company. He'd lost the offices and he had let all of his employees go. Yet, for the past six months, he had managed to make it as a lone guy doing everything himself. Along with the sleep deprivation and the stacking hospital bills and the endless hours of searching for a door to knock on when it came to work, Kevin had managed to keep some money coming in.

Precision Design was not dead.

"I always feared the worst," he said.

"That's what you do."

He leaned over and held her hand. It felt good to touch her, to have a moment when it was just the two of them.

"You know," Kevin said, "for so long, I've been in this fight. This fight with the rest of the world. All about building and climbing and maintaining and all that. And it's just—it's utter nonsense."

"You had—you have a good company."

There was Jenny's confidence again. It was a beautiful thing.

"But it's the journey. A never-ending journey. And when I left that building thinking that Precision was done, I felt—I felt relieved. I felt like some gigantic burden was lifted."

Jenny raised her eyebrows. "Some of those burdens are still here."

"I'm not saying the burden of my responsibilities suddenly went away. But I just—"

He turned toward Jenny and took her hand.

“You want to know the second-best thing that happened to me last year? After being able to hold our twins and meet them for the first time?”

“What?”

“It was—this might sound crazy—but it was getting that Golden Ticket.”

Jenny didn’t know what he was talking about. Of course she didn’t.

But I asked God for one and that was exactly what He gave me, what He gave us.

“I started thinking about this business trip, and I realized that there’s only one reason it’s happening. That got me thinking about other things. Remember back in January when everything was chaotic and—”

“I don’t remember the first three months of the year,” Jenny said with a smile.

“No, I know. But remember how I felt awful that we hadn’t gone to Kaylee’s Christmas program. I’d felt bad after seeing her and getting the invitation.”

“But we’ve been to four of her shows this spring. And that’s *after* having the babies. Your sister should be happy.”

“That’s just it—I would have missed those. And the fact that I’ve actually started going back to church—I think a big reason for that was seeing Bruce again and starting to hang out with him.”

“So what’s with the magical ticket?”

“The Golden Ticket,” Kevin said, correcting her. “It was picking up that paper angel for the kid named Thomas. ’Cause every single thing that happened—every time I went to buy something—I ended up seeing someone. Kaylee. Pastor Bruce. Or even Amanda."

"Wait—that's how you ended up coming across the woman at the Opryland Hotel? The one who wants to start the new ad campaign?"

Hearing the awe in Jenny's voice brought on a wave of tingles over his body. He nodded and smiled. "I wish I could thank that Thomas."

Jenny looked at him. "He probably wishes the same."

"I wish he knew, you know?"

"It was a good thing, taking that paper angel."

"You were the one who told me to get one. And besides—it wasn't anything I did. It was an answer to prayer. And God doesn't answer me in subtle ways. He seems to do it in billboard fashion."

"Or times two," Jenny said.

He laughed. It was so peaceful for a moment. He thought of his upcoming drive to Nashville. He didn't want to leave Jenny and the boys.

"I don't want to waste any more time," Kevin said suddenly, surprising himself.

"You haven't wasted time. You haven't had any time to waste."

He gripped her hands tighter. "I want to make my life—make our lives count. I want them to matter. And outside of us taking care of those boys, and outside of me taking care of you, I want to do more."

"But what does that mean?"

Kevin sighed and shook his head, then looked up at the sky. "I don't know. I really don't. But I know something. Having God answer those prayers in such an amazing way—I just know that there's more I can do. I don't want to waste any more time on myself. I want every day to matter."

The monitor on the table lit up as the sound of one of the babies crying broke the peace.

"Well, I know what matters now," Jen said.

"I'll get him before I go."

He kissed her cheek and touched her shoulder, then stood up and went inside.

As he did, he thought there was still time in his life to do something grand. Something big. Something life-changing.

He entered the nursery and saw the two little faces staring up at him, and Kevin realized he already had done all of those things.

*

Lynn was too smart to subscribe to happily-ever-afters. Yet she was also ashamed to realize that she'd given up on them when her own son seemed to have been born with hope in his veins.

The choice didn't come after fasting and prayer. She wasn't a fasting-and-prayer sort of gal. God didn't speak to her at night or burn a bush in front of her windowsill. Instead, He spoke to her in simple yet sufficient ways.

Like a fortune cookie.

After Christmas, Daryl had called and written a dozen times, explaining that he was sober again, now attending AA meetings, describing how he was getting his life back in order, proving that he was truly trying to change. But all of that didn't matter because she was smart and she was stubborn.

Then one day she ordered the Mongolian beef, and the fortune cookie that came with it reminded her of Christmas.

The tiny strip of paper in her hand said the following:

"A small gift can bring joy to the whole family."

Lynn knew that it was true too.

The gifts that Thomas had given back at Christmas—the gifts that he had chosen to regive to others—had done something wonderful.

They had brought back her daughter's sweet smile.

They had forged a relationship between Thomas and the rest of the kids at school, not just the bullying basketball player who was jealous of the new kid.

They had helped her see herself in a different light when she glanced at pictures of her and the kids.

It had done all this but most importantly it had humbled and broken her husband.

It had been Daryl's final wake-up call.

In the form of a present.

And now she had a chance to do the same thing. To take her gift and give it back. To give something else, something more.

We're all given second chances. All of us.

The fortune cookie was right.

Before deciding, she had prayed about it and taken some time to know if she was making the right decision. There was stubbornness and then there was simple stupidity. Both were wrong in God's eyes, especially when it came to the kids. She just wanted to do the right thing.

It was over dinner one night at the trailer that she told them.

School had just gotten out and the summer stared down at them with its long, flashing eyes.

"Okay, so here's the deal," she said in a way that told them she didn't want them interrupting. "I've thought a lot about things. About our life here. About your father."

Lynn tightened her lips, wondering if she could go on. They both stared at her with an intensity that could only come from mentioning the word *father*.

"For some time now your father has been asking—begging—to see both of you. Saying that he's a changed person. Saying he wants to start over again. And every time I've heard it or read it, I've simply ignored it."

Lynn held a napkin in her hand. The plate in front of her still had fried chicken and mashed potatoes on it. She wasn't very hungry.

"The one thing I know—that I can't change—is that he's still your father. He'll always be your father. So I think that it's okay to see him. At least once this summer. To see how things are. To see how everything goes."

They knew what that meant. Neither of them had to ask for specifics.

"I wasn't sure if this was the right decision," she continued. "But then it hit me the last time I spoke with him. Your father said he wanted to pick up the pieces and start over. I got angry at him. I'd been thinking about that for some time until I realized this. Some pieces aren't meant to be picked up and patched back together. Some pieces are meant to stay broken and left where they belong."

"Mom—"

"Wait," she told Thomas, knowing that he might disagree with her. "Just wait. I believe that. Sometimes, like in our case, it's impossible to just 'start over.' That's a fairy tale. Yet I do believe that it's possible to start again without that baggage. You leave the hurt and the pain on the side of the road like scraps from a car crash. You don't throw them away because you need to remember. Yet at the same time you realize that you're still alive and still in one piece and that God's given you a chance to keep going down that road. So you keep driving and you see where the road takes you."

"Are we going to move back in with him?" Sara asked.

"No," Lynn said. "All I'm going to promise your father is this. That we're willing to see him this summer. It starts there. And then—we'll see."

"We'll see what?" Sara asked.

"We'll see."

*

Some roads were made of dirt and dust and remain unnamed. They didn't see many fancy cars and didn't get much use. But they were still valuable because they were still going somewhere.

As the car stopped in front of the freshly painted house in the middle of this back road to nowhere, Thomas couldn't help but remember their leaving a year and a half ago. That was a different story and a different destination.

The new paint seemed to match the new story.

It took him a few minutes before he saw what waited for them on the porch.

There were a dozen gifts in silver and gold baking in the sun.

Seeing the gifts made him smile. Especially the new bicycle resting against the house with a big bow attached to its shiny exterior.

Thomas liked to believe. He liked to think that every dusty road could lead to somewhere special. Not just a destination, but an experience. An experience and a purpose.

He liked to think that it wasn't about the destination.

He'd always believed that he—that *they*—could make something out of nothing, right alongside this dirty, dusty road.

Climbing out of the car, then seeing the face of the man who called himself Dad, Thomas knew he had a chance to do something special.

This was one more gift he'd been given.

A chance to forgive.

To forgive and to start again.

Acknowledgments

I'd like to thank:

God for the gift of experience.

My sister Patricia. She's always been my light.

Tenacity Management. Extra love to Jenny Bohler.

O'Neil Hagaman.

William Morris.

My family and friends.

All the sponsors who chose a Paper Angel from the tree and made sure my sister and I had a great Christmas when we were kids. I'll never forget you!

My fans . . . I could not do what I do without you! You help me help our most valuable and vulnerable resource, our children! I'm very thankful for you!

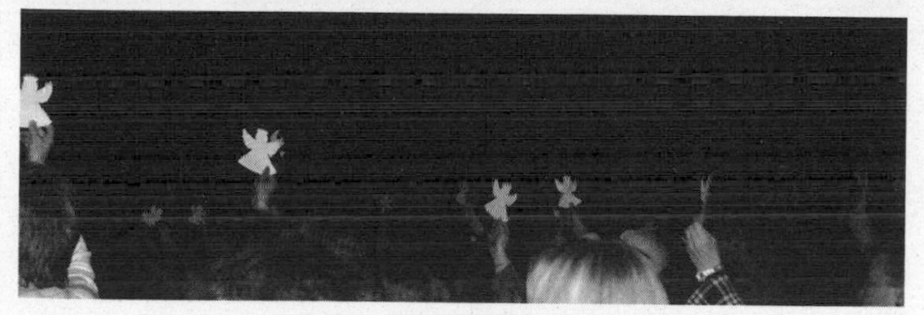

Photo courtesy of Dawn McDonald

Author's Note

I was performing at a charity event in my hometown back in North Carolina in March 2006. During the song "Paper Angels" I asked the audience to participate. They sang softly; then one by one they began holding these handmade paper angels in the air. Eventually the entire arena was glowing with paper angels waving side to side as the audience sang louder and louder. It was a spiritual sight. After the show, a girl handed me one of these handmade paper angels and said, "It took me a long time to make these. I hope you like them." I taped that paper angel to the back of my guitar, where it has remained to this day.

For more information regarding
The Salvation Army Angel Tree program,
please visit www.salvationarmyusa.org.

Jimmy Wayne is the national spokesperson for CASA.
For more information, please visit their Web site:
www.CASAforChildren.org.

Jimmy started his Meet Me Halfway campaign in January 2010 to raise awareness for youth who "age out" of the foster care system and face serious life problems such as homelessness and poverty. Please visit www.projectMMH.org to see how you can help.